CATHERINE LIM

The Howling Silence

Cover design by Lorraine Aw

First published 1999 by Horizon Books

This edition published 2017 by Marshall Cavendish Editions
An imprint of Marshall Cavendish International

Other Marshall Cavendish Offices:
Marshall Cavendish Corporation. 99 White Plains Road, Tarrytown NY 10591-9001, USA • Marshall Cavendish International (Thailand) Co Ltd. 253 Asoke, 12th Flr, Sukhumvit 21 Road, Klongtoey Nua, Wattana, Bangkok 10110, Thailand • Marshall Cavendish (Malaysia) Sdn Bhd, Times Subang, Lot 46, Subang Hi-Tech Industrial Park, Batu Tiga, 40000 Shah Alam, Selangor Darul Ehsan, Malaysia

National Library Board, Singapore Cataloguing-in-Publication Data

Name(s): Lim, Catherine, author.
Title: The howling silence : tales of the dead and their return / Catherine Lim.
Other title(s): Tales of the dead and their return
Description: Singapore : Marshall Cavendish Editions, [2017]
Identifier(s): OCN 993267085 | ISBN 978-981-4779-54-8 (paperback)
Subject(s): LCSH: Short stories, Singaporean (English).
Classification: DDCS823—dc23

Printed in Singapore by JCS Digital Solutions Pte Ltd

CONTENTS

"There are more things in
heaven and earth, Horatio,
than are dreamt of in your philosophy."

Great-grandfather with Teeth

During a vacation from my studies in the United States in 1992, I decided to spend the night alone in the old, abandoned family house at Pek Joo Street, one in a row of dilapidated shophouses that must have been built before the turn of the century, soon to be torn down to make way for a gleaming shopping complex.

The reasons behind my decision were two: sentiment and bravado. The sentiment concerned my birth in one of the three bedrooms on the upper floor, which still contained the birth-bed, an old, carved, monstrous piece of furniture. The bravado concerned the alleged population of ghosts in the house, which I was determined to confront, alone and unaided, so that I could regale friends with vivid telling of the experience later. No. 37 was said to be the most haunted of the houses on Pek Joo Street; passers-by could feel the odour of its unsanctity.

"It's definitely unclean," they shuddered. Strange sounds, shadowy presences, fleeting movements – all had been heard or sighted in the derelict house of my birth.

The ghosts were those not only of forebears who had lived and died there, but also of maid servants sold into bondage to the family. The last ancestor to die was the first to be born there, my great-grandfather, Tan Siong Teck, who died at eighty, just months before I was born, his first great-grandson. The only existing photograph of him, yellowed with age, shows a handsome, robust, well-built old man with a perfect set of teeth. In those days of stiff, formal poses for the camera, people never smiled. Great-grandfather did, for the pure pleasure, I was told, of showing off those marvellous octogenarian teeth.

"Tell me about *Chor Kong*," I used to ask my mother when I was a little boy, impressed by the fact that he exited the world just as I entered it. But my mother would look displeased and turn away each time, as from a horrible secret not fit to be told. Great-grandfather became an absorbing mystery to me.

Two maidservants had died in the house, one of whom a nineteen-year-old called Ah Kum, had hanged herself from a ceiling beam one cold dawn before anybody was awake.

I relished the prospect when back in the States after my vacation, of tantalising my college mates, especially my roommate, Bryan Roberts, a dry, cynical Business Studies student, with a cool, detailed description of ' My Adventures in the Haunted Ancestral Home'.

"I spent a night with the spirits of my forebears, apologising sincerely, on behalf of the Singapore Urban Redevelopment Authority, for the rude expulsion from their home, and promising to help them, in whatever way I could, in their resettlement in a new home. On behalf of the government, I offered at least a million dollars in compensation, burning ten stacks of ghost money until everything was properly reduced to ashes. It is said that some spirits do not even know that they are dead, and wander around in a confused state for years, on the face of the earth. I showed extra sympathy for these poor benighted souls which surely included that

of my great-grandfather, a fine-looking old man who must have done horrible things in life to make his descendants too fearful to even mention his name. As for the spirits of the suicides, they are supposed to be the most tormented of all. So I had to be extra gentle with that poor maidservant Ah Kum whose body, when it was detached from the hanging rope, was found to be with child. I was therefore dealing with two distressed spirits, not one; no pair of ghosts could be more tragic than those of mother and unborn child."

I already saw Bryan Roberts' jaw dropping. He often spoke patronisingly about the bizarre customs of the East, in particular the obsession with the supernatural. I would rub that in, and watch his reaction with perverse delight.

My mother said, "Kwan, I wish you wouldn't." (She never called me by my Western name, Rudolph.) I had told her of my plan, and she had appeared upset by it. She went on to say severely, "Don't go disturbing them or making fun of them. They can be dangerous. What's the matter with you?" She never referred to ghosts by any other term than a safe pronoun. She also probably regretted my Western education which had given me a Western name she could not pronounce, a Western religion she could not understand and a Western levity she could not condone.

"Kwan, light these joss-sticks for *Chor Kong*," she said, placing them in my hand. She was clearly worried that my frivolity had displeased the ancestors who must be appeased quickly. But I could not make myself do it. That gesture of appeasement would have a hollow ring to it.

That night, alone in the family house on Pek Joo Street, I saw the ghost of an old man. Strangely, I was unafraid. Perhaps it was my ability to stay detached from the culture of my childhood, to watch it coolly from the outside and not be intimidated by the exotic ghosts, ghouls and graveyard trysts that had so frightened me as a child. Indeed, I was elated at the thought of having a *real* supernatural experience, one actually independent of my imagination, that I could later narrate to my Western friends in every authenticity of detail.

I was lying on the bed of my birth when it happened. I heard small rustling sounds and instantly sat up to see an old man standing at the foot of my bed staring at me. He was thin and stooped, with wisps of white hair on his head. He was wearing a short-sleeved, white singlet and black cotton trousers. All these details registered clearly in the dim light of a street lamp coming through the wooden window slats. From the outside world too came the sound of cats snarling and of a garbage bin overturning, as if to confirm to me that what I was experiencing was not a dream but reality.

The ghost stared at me for a long time and I looked back, still unafraid. He moved slightly and opened his mouth, as if to tell me something. It was at this point that I saw, with a start, that he had no teeth. A toothless ghost. Even while gazing awe-struck at him, I was aware of the literal and metaphorical comicality of the situation. His gums were completely bare. It was almost as if, as a joke he had appeared with the precise purpose to disclose that special feature. Then he vanished.

The next morning I told my mother about the ghost. She became very agitated, shaking her head vigorously. She said, "I told you, but you wouldn't listen." What she meant was that I had, by my reckless deed, tampered with the past which now, like a disturbed pool, was stirring with dark, ugly secrets.

"Who was the old man?" I said.

"Your great-grandfather," said my mother. Great-grandfather of the robust, well-built body and perfect teeth? Or did ghosts continue to suffer the ravages of time in the other world, becoming older, greyer, feebler?

"It was your *Chor Kong*," my mother repeated, and was of course compelled to tell the horrible tale she had been holding back for so many years.

Great-grandfather Tan Siong Teck, up to the eightieth and last year of his life, had never even suffered a minor ailment like a cough or cold. His good health was legendary, which he would proudly proclaim every morning to the world through an hour's exercise of *tai chi* in an open piece of ground at the back of the house. Neighbours stopped to watch admiringly. While other old men and women drooped, shuffled, limped, wheezed and used walking sticks, Great-grandfather strode briskly about, always wearing a short-sleeved white cotton singlet and black cotton trousers, the best exemplar of the much desired longevity and good health enshrined in every Chinese greeting.

But the greatest source of his pride and pleasure was his teeth: Great-grandfather never visited a dentist in all his life. He scorned to use anything but charcoal powder for cleaning that prized feature, carefully applying the stuff on every tooth and rubbing it vigorously with his forefinger. Then he rinsed his mouth several times with clear, clean fresh water from a large tin mug. He spat out the water, in dark streams, into a drain, watched by fascinated children. For their benefit, he clowned about, baring his charcoal-blackened teeth to frighten them and rinsing his mouth with loud, exaggerated sloshing sounds. The elaborate ritual of teeth-cleaning was always followed by the pulling out of a small mirror from a trouser pocket. Carefully examining his teeth, now white and sparkling in the mirror,

Great-grandfather would amuse the children further by inviting them to come up for a closer look. Once someone gave him a tube of Pepsodent toothpaste. Great-grandfather threw it away in disdain.

His pride and vanity about his teeth made him overly critical about other people's. He laughed unkindly at the brown, rotting stumps of Ah Chow, a neighbour who was a good fifteen years younger. He pointed with spiteful glee at the three remaining teeth wobbling precariously on the lower jaw of Ah Poon Soh who sold vegetables at the market. Ah Poon Soh could no longer eat the pork she loved, and watched with good-natured envy as Great-grandfather cockily cracked open boiled chestnuts and crab claws with his excellent teeth.

Great-grandfather welcomed the visits of the itinerant dentist who came to the neighbourhood once a month, because he loved to watch, with childish fascination, bad teeth being yanked out by the dentist's brutal-looking spanner-like instrument, and the bloodied hollows being plugged with large wads of cotton wool. The dentist carried with him on his rounds a small spittoon into which yanked teeth and the used wads, soaking with blood, could be thrown. Great-grandfather even made fun of his own family members, none of whom had teeth that could remotely match his.

"*Siow*," they complained privately to each other, meaning that he was crazy and not behaving with the decorum and dignity expected with old age.

Then something happened. When Great-grandfather turned seventy-nine, one of his three sons, Second Granduncle Oon Hock, aged fifty-one, died of a mysterious illness. Only the day before, he was enjoying his usual drink of Guinness Stout in the coffeeshop three doors away. The next day, he complained of dizziness and asked his wife to rub Tiger Oil on his temples. She did so expertly and then went to get him a cup of hot Ovaltine. When she returned, he was slumped in his chair, dead.

Second Grand-aunt was inconsolable. After the funeral, when she had sufficiently calmed down, she made a sly remark to the effect that longevity for the old was fine, but should not be at the expense of the young. She had touched a raw nerve of the culture's abiding dilemma: what to do about old men and women who exceeded their appointment of long life, stealing years that should have been their children's. It was not in the natural order of things for parents to bury their children.

Second Grand-aunt, in her resentment, had planted the seeds of fear in that house on Pek Joo Street. It hung in the air, heavy, uneasy, palpable. It isolated Great-grandfather, already isolated by the eccentricities of his behaviour. But the old man, ever proud and stubborn, chose to ignore the snide remarks and continued his healthy regimen of daily morning exercise and meticulous teeth cleaning. He was looking forward to his eightieth birthday the following year and to the eating of longevity noodles at the celebration dinner which his children and grandchildren were obliged, by filial duty, to provide, and which was sure to confer at least another ten or fifteen years of good health.

Then another death in the family took place. This time it was a grandson, the youngest child of one of Great-grandfather's two daughters, First Aunt Kim Chee who lived at Downer Road, a few streets away. The boy, aged eleven, had fallen down while playing, slipped into a coma and died within a week. His frantic parents had consulted one temple medium after another for a cure, but in vain. First a son, now a grandson. The old man's longevity was proving to be a curse in the family;

it was dangerously extending itself by eating up the life-years of progeny. A relative went to consult a fortune teller who instantly identified the specific source of the continuing evil: Great-grandfather's teeth. They were abnormal teeth, too long, too strong, too powerful, indicating a monstrous appetite. They were the teeth of perverted parenthood that would devour its own flesh and blood. How many more offspring would have to be sacrificed? Great-grandfather's perfect teeth had suddenly become the focus of everyone's resentment and fear.

Since the gods sternly forbade any disrespect for the old, this resentment could only be expressed indirectly. The aggrieved victims, Second Grand-aunt and First Aunt Kim Chee, singly or together, made caustic remarks to neighbours who were certain to pass them on to the hateful old one.

Great-grandfather seethed with anger. He felt all the pain of the insult as well as all the confusion of an ambiguous gift from the gods: had the teeth of longevity turned into a weapon of destruction in his own family? Had the prized symbol of his good health become a toxic gift?

In his confused state, he became peevish and quarrelsome, isolating himself even more. As his birthday approached, he said loudly and testily, "No need for any celebration. Why bother at all?" It was of course unthinkable that the august eightieth birthday of an aged parent would go uncelebrated, that the longevity noodles would not be cooked and eaten by everybody.

At that time, my mother, who was married to one of Great-grandfather's grandsons (my father died when I was nine), was pregnant with me. A son, a grandson, a great-grandson: would the savage teeth chomp through three generations? My mother, a young bride at nineteen, was terrified. She avoided looking at Great-grandfather. Whenever she passed him, she looked down, and raised her hands instinctively to cover her swelling belly, to protect the unborn great-grandson. She had begun her married life at 37, Pek Joo Street, a house with only three bedrooms and an endlessly proliferating family. At one stage, the family spilled over into the adjoining house at No. 38, which happened to be vacant, by simply breaking down a separating wall.

On the special day of Great-grandfather's eightieth birthday, at the precise hour when the food was all laid out on the table to be eaten, with a huge plate of celebratory noodles in the centre, Great-grandfather was nowhere to be seen. The children were sent to look for him. Someone had seen him, hours earlier, in the toolshed at the back, fiddling with tools and making strange noises. Nobody remembered seeing him doing his exercise in the morning or cleaning his teeth. Everybody became worried. What had happened to Great-grandfather?

Then somebody whispered, "Ssh, he's coming!" and the family quickly took their places at the long table, silent and anxious. They watched nervously as Great-grandfather came in, looking paler than usual, and took his place at the head of the table. Then he began to help himself to the longevity noodles.

It was at this point that the family realised something was wrong. They looked at him in horror, or rather, at his mouth, as it opened wide to eat the noodles. For there were no teeth. The gums were totally bare, and still bleeding from the despoliation, probably with a spanner from the toolshed. (A child later discovered all the teeth, a very large number, thrown into an old tin bucket in the shed, in a mess of blood, spittle and old rags.) Great-grandfather ate the noodles slowly, drawing in each long strand carefully, so as to maintain its length and wholeness, as tradition required. One by one, each long, wet, slippery noodle was sucked into the toothless mouth and swallowed, with great slurping noises. Then when he had finished, Great-grandfather looked at the faces around the table, looked at each long and lingeringly. He said nothing but his eyes were bright with savage triumph: *Are you all satisfied now?*

He turned to my mother and looked hard at her, and again it was his eyes that did the talking: *Your unborn child is safe, Granddaughter-in-law. If anything happens, remember I'm not to blame. The young must not always blame the old. I've done my best.*

My mother said it was the most horrible moment in her life. Once again, she had instinctively placed both hands on her growing stomach to protect me from the malevolent stare.

Great-grandfather died soon after. It would appear that with his prized teeth gone, he had nothing more to live for. He lost interest in life, refused all food and medicine and went into rapid decline, dying only two months after his eightieth birthday. He was a shadow of his former self.

I went back to the house at No.37, Pek Joo Street. I wanted to see Great-grandfather's ghost again, this time to thank him. He had laid down his teeth for me. For this I would first beg forgiveness from the ghost and then thank him with the fullness of a humble, chastened heart. I waited all night and when dawn broke, the time for the spirits to return to their abodes, I knew Great-grandfather would never come again. He had left No.37, Pek Joo Street, forever.

Before I returned to the States, I paid a visit to the Shining Light Temple in which his ashes are kept. The Kong Seng Cemetery where he had been buried had been cleared for industrial development in 1984. Great-grandfather's grave, together with hundreds of others, had been duly exhumed, and the remains collected by one of my uncles for cremation and final resting in an urn in the Shining Light Temple.

Lighting two joss-sticks to stick in front of Great-grandfather's urn, I felt an urge to talk to him. I would have much preferred a ghost, palpable and real, in the urgency of its brief visiting time, to a cold, silent urn with its cold ashes. I stood awkwardly before the urn, one among hundreds in neat rows, and was not sure what to say, the great-grandson from a world separated from his by a howling, immeasurable gulf. But for one brief moment on a dark night in the old house at 37, Pek Joo Street, we had managed to reach across that gulf.

In Lieu of a Dream

On 27 August 1990, I got engaged to Paul Ratnam, after we finally overcame a whole phalanx of obstacles, too tedious to describe, related to our different ethnic, cultural and religious backgrounds. (All I will say is that we offended our respective families so much that they refused to have anything to do with us.) it was an engagement party "with a difference", as Paul would say, meaning it was held on impulse, only two friends were present, and there was no engagement ring, only a promise of it. Paul, who travelled a lot in his work for an international investment company, said he would buy me a ring from Paris. There would be a second engagement party, he said, and several wedding parties, to match the number of obstacles cleared. That was Paul: unconventional, unpredictable, fun-loving, lovable.

On 3 September, on his way home from Paris, the plane he was in, together with a hundred and fifty other passengers, crashed into a river in a remote part of Malaysia. There were no survivors; that is always the next most fearful announcement. There could not have been any survivors in that treacherous plunge straight from the sky into the Sungei Mati, appropriately named the River of Death.

It was amazing how hope defied reality. All of us, family, relatives, loved ones who rushed over to the site of the disaster as soon as the authorities made the necessary arrangements, were united by the ferocity of hope that demolished or suspended all reason and logic to challenge the stark truth of the newspaper and other media reports. As we flew in a government-provided plane and then rode in buses and vans through rough jungle country, pale and stricken, we clung to the vision of our beloved ones among those survivors now swimming helplessly about in the river or wandering about in a dazed state in the jungle or being taken care of by kind villagers in a remote *kampung*, and prayed fervently. "Hold on a little while longer, we're coming." Hope held till the moment we reached the spot of the crash for then we saw, to our horror, the cruelly vast expanse of the river and its pitiless murky depths, against which no man or machine would stand a chance.

Then grief took over. Absorbed by my own numbing pain, I was vaguely aware of the spread of bereavement's need for a shared outpouring on the site of the communal sorrow; one by one, the bereaved ones began to cry, sob, cling to each other, call out the name of the beloved. I shed no tears, but stood staring dully at the lazily churning water of the River Mati. My sister, Siok Woon, had accompanied me on this trip; she stood by my side all the time, holding my arm.

After it was all over and we returned home, to face an anguished time of private grief and unwanted public attention, personal confusion over the mysterious circumstances surrounding the crash and the endless, noisy media coverage of it, I recollected vividly some scenes that at the time were only vague impressions – a woman throwing flower petals into the water and calling out name "Yuen! Yuen!", a family, all in white T-shirts and black pants, chanting prayers and lighting joss-sticks beside a plate of oranges and a bowl of candy, an elderly man sobbing his heart out and threatening to throw himself into the river, held back by a young man and woman weeping silently, a young girl, pale and distraught, clutching a photo of her family, her parents and four younger siblings, all wiped out.

For days I wandered about the house in a numbed state, attended to by my anxious sister. She wanted me to talk, say anything, scream, cry, and watched nervously as I maintained my stoic silence. I read all the reports about the crash in the local newspapers, as well as those in the foreign press. There was one particular report which attracted my attention. It was only a small paragraph about how, without exception, all those who had visited the site, had begun to have dreams of their loved ones buried in the unyielding depths of the River Mati. The report said that the dreams were mainly peaceful ones and brought much comfort. One woman said she saw her son in a kind of boat drifting gently down the river and waving to her. He was saying something, which she could not hear, but it must have been something happy, for he was smiling. Another woman said that in her dream, which was extremely vivid, her husband stood beside her on the river bank as she was gazing at the water, put his arm around her, and told her not to worry but to take good care of the children and his aged father, before fading away. Yet another woman, a young executive whose boyfriend was on his way to Singapore to spend a holiday with her, saw him walking towards her then embracing her.

It was grossly inaccurate report; I wanted to call the reporter to say angrily, "'Without exception', did you say? Well let me tell you *I* didn't have any dream. If you had taken the trouble to contact all of us –"

Then I realised that *the anger was not against the reporter but Paul.* Why hadn't he done like the others who had appeared to their grieving ones to comfort and console? Would it have been so difficult to appear just once, to talk to me, touch me, tell me everything was all right?

My sister said, "Now, that's not fair, Ching. You know Paul never subscribed to those things. And neither do you." Those 'things' were the beliefs in the supernatural phenomena of dreams, visitations, the return of the dead, which Paul and I, priding ourselves in our rationality, had little patience with.

"Just one dream," I persisted. "Couldn't he have just come once? That would have meant so much." It was no longer reason talking; it was the desperation born of need and hope. I began to envy all those who had dreams of their beloved dead.

I do not know how I survived those months; I returned to work and received the visits of family and friends and even attended a social function or two. But deep inside was the numbed centre, no longer responsive, but aching with a hope that refused to be dulled with time. I went to sleep each night with the hope and got up dispirited by its continuing non-fulfilment.

The anniversary of the crash came around, and I decided to make a second visit to the site, to stand on the banks of the River Mati for a few minutes of quiet reflection. I thought if Paul didn't wish to some to me, I would go to him instead. And this time, I politely and firmly turned down Siok Woon's offer to accompany me.

As soon as I arrived at the site, an unspeakable sadness descended upon me. I stood forlornly on a quiet spot on the bank and looked at the ugly, slowly stirring waters. There was an old man in a boat who was fishing with some poles and a net. A year ago, all fishing activity had been suspended while expert teams sent by the authorities trawled almost the entire river bed for debris of the crash. I had not wanted to look at the twisted pieces of wreckage brought out and laid on the river bank; now I looked on desultorily as the old fisherman puled in his net and searched for fish among a small mound of mud and rotting leaves.

I must have stood on the river bank for half an hour. As I got ready to go, I heard a voice and turned to see the old man tying his boat to a tree stump on the river bank and signalling to me to wait. He came up and handed me something. It was a small box, its red velvet still visible under the river mud. I took it and opened it. *A ring. A diamond engagement ring. On the box was the name of the Paris jeweller.*

A coincidence. The ring had been lost in the water and found by a fisherman. I *happened* to be there and the fisherman *happened* to know I was the fiancée and had duly returned it to me. The fisherman, eking out a miserable living, *happened* to not understand the value of the diamond, or understanding, refused to let need stand in the way of nobility.

A coincidence? To call that happening that late morning on the banks of the River Mati on 3 September 1991 a coincidence would be the grossest insult to tenderness' gift from beyond the grave.

Song of Mina

There is a part of District 32, one of the oldest districts in Singapore, in which all the streets are named after flowers – Bougainvillea Street, Frangipani Street, Orchid Street, Balsam Lane, Canna Close, Hibiscus Avenue – as if a colonial administrator in those bygone days, charmed by the exotic tropical blooms of his new home, had decided to officially commemorate their beauty.

But for modern-day Singapore, the streets are better known for sheer squalor. They contain the most notorious brothels in Singapore, a virtual moral cesspit, in the midst of a clean, thriving, hardworking, prosperous society. There is talk that soon the area – dubbed the Red Red District, in testimony to the virulence of its activities rather than to the floral brilliance of its street names – will be cleared and cleaned up for a vast complex of business and residential properties. Right now, life goes on as usual among jaded prostitutes ready to settle for a few dollars from their clients, generally impoverished, desperate men, both old and young, crawling out of the dank woodwork of their failed lives, smashed dreams, twisted desires.

There is an old, crumbling two-storey hotel-brothel on Orchid Street going by the resonantly beautiful name of Song of the Forest, that used to be managed by a woman who, not to be outdone by the dazzling nomenclature all around her, called herself Bunga Mas. Bunga Mas is sixty-five years old and continues to wear the make-up and hairstyle that must have been her trademark when she was working in the brothel in her youth. She would have continued to wear the same clothes, except that she has grown fat; indeed, it is an obesity so gross it makes people look away uncomfortably. Bunga Mas, with her extraordinarily vivid make-up, ridiculously girlish curls that cluster tightly on her forehead and around her ears, and the screaming bright colours of her long tent dresses, spends her time sitting in a coffeeshop near the hotel, drinking coffee interminably, looking at passers-by and challenging them to look at her, telling stories to whoever cares to listen. Her favourite story is of a young prostitute called Mina who was found murdered on her bed one night in 1976, and whose ghost continues to haunt the hotel. The murder can be verified, because it was reported in the newspapers, but not the haunting, for nobody in the brothel has ever seen a ghost, and those who have seen it don't know it's a ghost and cannot be told, because it will be bad for business. (Mina's murderer was found, tried and executed in 1977.)

As a reporter, I am always on the prowl for interesting stories. Having heard of Bunga Mas' story, I hurried to meet her. Ghost or no ghost, Bunga Mas, with her very colourful life, would prove excellent material for a captivating article. The trouble is that my editor throws out most of my stories as "unsuitable", meaning that they are too frivolous or sensational or plain nonsense. Recently she threw out my Mina story as the greatest nonsense she has ever read, but she says she may consider a piece on Bunga Mas if, at some future time, she decided to run a frank series of articles on "the other side" of Singapore. I'll keep my Mina story for myself.

"How do you know her ghost haunts the hotel?" I ask Bunga Mas. I have treated her to a beer and she is in a very expansive and talkative mood. She smiles, looks at me and suddenly brightens up with an idea. "Come to the Song of the Forest at nine," she says with a wink. "I'll be waiting for you."

Me, a cub reporter, fresh-faced, roving around in T-shirt, jeans or denim skirt, sandals or sneakers, going to a brothel? My mother would die of fright if I told her.

At the appointed time, I am at the Song of the Forest. Bunga Mas is waiting for me, clad in a bright purple cotton tent. She appears at ease, in familiar surroundings. She introduces me to a middle-aged man with bad teeth, called Lek, who is the hotel-keeper and her friend, amiable enough to go along with any scheme for the benefit of a young, curious reporter.

"We're waiting," says Bunga Mas. "It's usually about this time." I look both of them quizzically but decide not to ask questions. I wait with them.

Then, as if on cue, a man comes in. He is about forty. He is wearing a red T-shirt and black trousers. He is carrying a helmet under his arm, so he must have come on a motorcycle. Looking at him, I cannot tell what his educational background is, nor his occupation. He speaks some English.

"You listen carefully," Bunga Mas whispers to me. The man says, a little shyly, "I'd like to see the lady at the upstairs window."

Bunga Mas says casually, "Which one of them? Describe her," giving the impression that at the Song of the Forest, the client begins with a selection from a row of women exhibited at the upstairs open windows. The man, growing red with embarrassment, describes her. Long hair. Fair. Blue dress. A red flower in her hair. He is clearly taken up by her beauty, although he is too shy to mention it.

"You mean Mina," Bunga Mas says matter-of-factly. "She's not available. Would you like someone else?"

The man frowns. He looks puzzled and a little annoyed. "What do you mean not available? I just saw her, standing at the window."

"I tell you she's not available," says Bunga Mas. "You can go upstairs if you like and see for yourself. But would you like to meet Rosie –"

The man leaves in a hurry. Bunga Mas says that this has been the pattern for the last twenty years – a man coming in with the eager request, then being told that the beautiful woman he has just seen is not available, has just left, has just fallen ill, etc, etc.

For every year, on the anniversary of her murder. Mina's ghost appears, always standing at the window, in full view of the men passing below. Enchanted, they come looking for her, but she vanishes as soon as they step in. there is no trace of her. Only once has there been a faint whiff of the distinctive perfume she use to wear.

Some of the men do not go away but insist on a search. They go away more puzzled than ever and sometimes shout angrily at the hotel staff for playing a stupid trick on them.

Of course the hotel staff cannot tell them the truth. That will ruin business. They will be terrified to come to a brothel in which a prostitute had been found murdered on her bed, her naked body so brutally mutilated that the police, according to the newspaper report, said that they had never encountered a more grisly murder. The men will be even more terrified if they were told that the prostitute's ghost returns to the hotel every year, on the anniversary of the murder, and stands at an open window smiling.

Bunga Mas has a theory. She thinks that the ghost has been coming back with a specific purpose – revenge. It is not enough for the ghost that her murderer had been executed for his crime. The heinous deed calls for continuing punishment. Those related to him must pay too. One day, his son will pass by the Song of the Forest, look up and see the beautiful Mina at the window. He will come in looking for her. This time, she will not vanish but wait for him. When they are by themselves, she will take her final revenge. She will make sure he dies a more horrible death than hers, for his father's death by the executioner's noose, was brief and painless, and therefore inadequate. After this final revenge, Mina's ghost will be at peace at last and will no longer come to the Song of the Forest.

I am fired by this strange story and boldly ask Bunga Mas if I may go upstairs and stand by the window where Mina's ghost has just stood. I have never seen a ghost; standing at the spot of its recent visitation may be just as exciting.

"I wouldn't, if I were you," says Bunga Mas with a shudder.

Temple of the Little Ghosts

Do babies have souls? Do aborted foetuses, never given the chance to reach their term, become ghosts that come back to haunt their murderous mothers?

My best friend – let us call her Rosalind – thinks so. She says that they not only come back but make their presence felt and heard during every waking and sleeping hour so that their mothers become mad with guilt.

There is a definite streak of theatricality in Rosalind.

"How does that square with your beliefs as a Roman Catholic?" I challenge. "Souls, yes, but revengeful ghosts? Your church surely doesn't share the primitive beliefs of your ancestors?"

Rosalind and I are such close friends that we can speak our minds freely and bluntly to each other. We were in school and university together, sharing an intense love for literature, especially Shakespeare. She converted to the Catholic religion when she was an undergraduate, forsaking what she called the dark murky world of ancestral spirits and sinister temple deities such as the Monkey God and the Lightning God for the calm, reassuring, radiant world of Christianity.

During our years in the university, Rosalind used to regale

me with stories of that strange world of her ancestors. After her conversion to the Catholic religion, she became obsessed with what she said must be the ugliest taint in her family history – the systematic practice of abortion, so strongly condemned by her church, carried on by the entire female line, from her mother backwards through her grandmother, great-grandmother and forebears lost in the mists of the remote past, way back to the ancestral village in southern China. A very old servant in the family who had come from China eighty years ago once told Rosalind that as a girl, she had on one occasion witnessed the death of a newborn baby girl who was smothered with rags, and on another, seen the body of a tiny infant, half buried in the mud of the rice-field. Abortion was not as heinous as infanticide, Rosalind said, but considering that God had already breathed life and soul into a foetus from the moment of its conception, it was bad enough.

"Oh the barbaric primitivism makes me shudder," said Rosalind. She told me that her great-grandmother, who was the first to come from China to settle in Penang (Rosalind's mother was born in Singapore), had used certain traditional medicines, mixed with the ashes of burnt prayer paper. Once something went wrong and she was ill with a high fever for days. The next female down the line, Rosalind's grandmother, also relied on the traditional herbal brews as well as the services of a native *kampung* woman whose skilful hands did the job by a special method of massaging the stomach and the womb. This forebear was desperate enough to try any recommended method, including the insertion of opium pellets. Once she bled for days and thought she would die. As for Rosalind's mother, she refused to talk about her methods, apart from saying that it involved the eating of young green pineapple, washed down with beer. As a little girl, Rosalind remembered a time when her mother was mysteriously ill for days, vomiting continuously.

Why was abortion so freely practised in her family? Rosalind said that the root of the problem was the remarkable fecundity of the women, combined with the equally remarkable appetite of the men. If there had been no control of the number of children born from this awesome conjunction of lust and receptivity, there have been a proliferation beyond any ability of parents to feed, house and clothe. Despite the systematic abortions, Rosalind's great-grandmother had eleven children, her grandmother ten and her own mother seven.

"Didn't any of you have any feelings of guilt at all?" she once asked her mother. She had the horrible suspicion that each time a foetus had been successfully expelled from the body, it was just one more piece of detritus to be thrown away in a rubbish bin or gutter. Her mother said tersely, "Your new religion is yours, my ancestors' beliefs are mine." The urgent need to feed and take care of living children left no time or energy for guilt over dead ones.

Rosalind shuddered at the barbarity of it all, but took heart by something which her mother, in a more communicative and amenable mood, told her. There was a neighbour, a Buddhist, who, having helped at least a dozen women get rid of their unborn, began to suffer the guilt of having wilfully destroyed life. Fearing to pay for the sin in the next life, she began a strict regimen of penitential cleansing and prayer in a temple, fasting and refraining from meat for thirty days. Another similarly guilt-stricken woman, the concubine of a rich *towkay* in Penang went back to her ancestral village in China, to build a temple dedicated to the soul of unborn babies, which became known as the Temple of the Little Ghosts. Many women went to pray at this temple to assuage the pain of their guilt, always returning with their peace of mind restored. Some of them left touching gifts at the Temple of Little Ghosts – cans of milk, feeding bottles, rubber teats, baby rattles, baby clothes. Rosalind never ceased to be fascinated by the quaintness of such stories, which she would tell me, with much theatrical colour.

After our university years together, we somehow lost touch with each other. As I later discovered, she had gone to the United States for a working stint. There she fell in love and lived with a man who turned out to be totally unsuitable. When she got pregnant, she decided to return home to Singapore, swearing she never wanted to see him again.

Back in Singapore, she went for a discreet abortion at a government hospital. There was none of the trauma of toxic opium pellets or raw unripe pineapple, none of the fear of bleeding to death. She was discharged from hospital the same day, taking her place among scores of young women returning quietly to college or office, grateful for the policy of a modern state that accepted the errancies of young people, helped them very discreetly to dispose of the fruit of their follies and in general spared them the misery of their less fortunate mothers and grandmothers.

Rosalind never told anybody about her secret. She only told me years later. When she met up with me again, our meeting was by pure accident. I was glad to see her again. She looked much thinner, but seemed anxious to rebuild her life, renting a comfortable little apartment to be on her own. She had returned, for solace, to the Catholic religion that she had briefly abandoned.

And then it happened. One evening, after Sunday mass in church, she returned home for a restful night before starting work the next day as a newly appointed assistant editor in a publishing company. It was a few minutes past midnight – "I knew the exact time, because I looked at the alarm clock on my bedside table" – when the noises began. Thinking it was a cockroach or a rat or some nocturnal insect, Rosalind prepared to go back to sleep. There was silence for a while – "About an hour, because when I looked at the clock again, it showed me one o'clock" – and then the noises started again. This time, they seemed very much closer. Switching on her bedside lamp, Rosalind began to look around the room, under her bed, behind the curtains, under her desk, still expecting to find cockroaches or rats. She became extremely puzzled when she noticed the noises ceased as soon as she switched on the light, but started all over again as soon as she got back to bed. Exasperated, she actually shouted out, "Whoever, whatever you are, will you please stop disturbing me?"

And it was at this point that she felt a sudden chill in the room. The chill permeated her body and caused her to shiver. She repeated, "Who are you? Will you please say something?" She waited in the darkness for an answer, and then it came. It was a small child's voice. "Mummy," it said. The voice sounded frightened and pleading. It said, "Mummy" again, then built up into a crescendo of terror, screaming "Mummy! Mummy!" She heard the voice dying away in the darkness, as if a crying child were being dragged away forcibly, while screaming for its mother.

Rosalind told me she could not sleep for the rest of the night. I asked the inevitable question, "Are you sure you were not just imagining it all?" After all, there had been the trauma of the abortion and the accompanying guilt.

"Three nights in a row?" said Rosalind. "I was a nervous

wreck and had to take medical leave. I had just begun work and was already asking to go on leave."

After the third night, the child's voice ceased. Then it came again, a week later. It was always the plaintive cry of the lost, abandoned child: "Mummy! Mummy!"

I asked Rosalind why she was so sure it was the baby she had aborted.

"I just knew," she said. "The cry pierced me, right to the deep core of something that would have been the bond between mother and child if I had allowed my baby to be born."

Rosalind went on a second round of confessions and penance with the priest of her church. But the cries of the child lost in the dark wilderness of a mother's secret shame continued. There was one night when she experienced more than a voice. She felt the touch of small, cold fingers on her face, the cold wet feel of naked baby flesh against her own. She woke up screaming.

I advised her to seek medical or psychiatric help.

Then suddenly I lost touch with her once more. She had disappeared. Her apartment was locked up, and the message on her answering machine said, "I will be away for a while. Please leave your name and phone number and I'll get back to you as soon as I can."

I waited anxiously for her return. One day, about a month after her disappearance, she called and asked to see me. I was relieved to see her again. She had gone shockingly thin, but seemed otherwise well and at peace with herself.

"Where on earth have you been?" I asked. I knew it had to do with the baby haunting.

She said, with a serenity of look I had not seen for a long time, "You know, I didn't think it would be like that. I felt such a deep peace in the grounds of that little temple! It took me a long time to find it; it's tucked away in a remote hillside village that can't be reached by bus or car. But I found it! And I've found my peace."

She had left no offerings of baby bottles or rubber comforters or toys at the Temple of Little Ghosts, only a simple note, written impulsively on the spot, in English, of a mother's profound sorrow, shame and remorse.

There is a perverseness in me that makes me ask the most insensitive questions. "Just how does all this square with your Roman Catholic beliefs?" I challenge. "You're more devout than ever, Rosalind, waking up every morning at five to attend mass. Yet you believe in baby ghosts and visit temples to appease them?"

Rosalind says quietly, "The mysteries of life and death are too great to be contained in any one religion." She continues, gazing reflectively into the distance, "'*There are more things in Heaven and Earth, Horatio, then are dreamt of in our philosophy.*'"

I see copies of her beloved Shakespeare on a shelf side by side with *The Tibetan Book of the Dead* and an impressive-looking tome called *The Psychology of Guilt.*

Rosalind tells me of a plan that is shaping in her mind. Since there is no organisation in Singapore to take up the rights of the unborn, she will go to the United States, live and work there and join an activist group called the Pro-lifers, in order to be able, should the small voice break through the darkness again to call her name, to respond with the sincerity of a contrition backed by real action.

The Colour of Solace

Julie did not dare say she had enjoyed herself at the Chandras' party, because her husband hadn't. Indeed, all the way home in the car, Tee Ngiam ranted and raged against the one person who had spoilt it all for him – Julie's best friend, Pek Yin, only eight months a widow but already laughing and flirting with the men. It was a violation of tradition's structures on proper widowhood. If Julie were brave enough, she would have said, "This is modern-day Singapore, you know," or "It's really none of your business, Ngiam." But she was never brave with her husband. Before his judgement, she retreated inwardly into the privacy of her own thoughts and feelings.

"That ridiculous dress," he said. She felt obliged to say something in agreement.

"Perhaps the bright colour didn't suit her," she ventured, and was instantly aware of a massive hypocrisy. For it was she who had persuaded Julie to buy that dress that day when they were shopping in Grace Boutique. Moreover, she had herself bought a similar one, in an even brighter shade of red. Of course she could never show it to him now; it would have to remain hidden in a corner of her closet.

"That ridiculous dress," Tee Ngiam repeated. It was worse

than improper widowhood; it was a desecration of the sanctity of marriage. "Half her breasts were showing." Julie suppressed a laugh at the thought of her husband, prim, stern, censorious, watching Pek Yin's décolletage.

"That slit up the side."

Clearly, every detail of the sexy, slinky, red dress had registered in Tee Ngiam's mind for the sole purpose of denouncing it later. Julie made a mental note to give away her dress to her sister, Annie.

It must have been loyalty to his dead colleague, Patrick Chang, that was causing all this resentment towards his widow. Patrick had died of cancer. At his funeral, Tee Ngiam, who delivered the eulogy, spoke feelingly about the dead man's sterling qualities. He was a filial son, a loving husband, a devoted father. And now his widow was defiling his memory. Again if Julie were brave, she would say, "But Pek Yin was just having fun. She's by nature a fun-loving person."

"Did you hear her referring to her old flame?"

So Pek Yin, the indefatigable party animal, the unstoppable chatterbox, had offended on another point. Tee Ngiam said that when his father died, his mother, who was only thirty-four then, was so loyal to his memory that she turned down several advantageous offers of marriage.

"Your father was a womaniser. You yourself told me how much your mother suffered. Who would have blamed her for having a life of her own after his death?" It was amazing how she could carry on these silent conversations in her head. In these silent conversations, she was actually impressed by her own clear logic and frank eloquence.

"To this day," said Tee Ngiam, "I hold my mother in the highest respect for that. Old flame indeed." His disgust with the frivolous widow had not yet worked itself out. And Julie made a second mental note – to throw away the postcard that she had received the day before from someone she had met while in college in England, so many years ago. By virtue of their two or three dates, Ron Whitten would be, in her husband's eyes, in that category of the obnoxious interloper called the "old flame". She would destroy the postcard straightaway, which was a pity, as she had been so pleasantly surprised by it and would have liked to send one to him in return.

Her husband had turned to her and said, "If I died, would you behave like this?" Husbands and wives tease one another about what they wish or do not wish their spouses to do or not to do, after their deaths, the magnanimous spouse urging quick remarriage to avoid loneliness, the possessive spouse threatening to come back as a ghost to haunt the remarried one, to use all its ghostly power to put an end to the shameful coupling with the new partner on the marital bed. Such playful bantering was not possible with Tee Ngiam.

He said again, "I'm asking you a serious question, Julie. Would you behave like Pek Yin so soon after my death?"

She was not so sure what was at issue – the insensitivity of the timing or the necessity for a permanent show of propriety by bereaved wives. She said immediately, "Of course not, Ngiam," having learnt to respond quickly, since hesitation only provoked the suspicion that she was hiding something.

He said, "My mother wore deep mourning black for my father for three years." In modern-day Singapore, no wife was expected to wear deep mourning black beyond the funeral. But as usual, the answer stayed locked in her throat. She sensed what he was going to say next.

"My reputation is important, Julie. Promise that you will not behave like Pek Yin after my death."

He measured loyalty in definite spans of mourning time. She was going to ask, "Eight months or three years?" but stopped. She felt a rising tide of irritation, but was able to say, without a hint of it, "Whatever you say, Ngiam."

"Is a year, two years, three years, too much for a man to ask his wife in return for – ?"

He could claim an even greater devotion than Patrick Chang. Through the twenty five years of their marriage, despite the childlessness, he had remained faithful, loyal and generous to her, extending his generosity to her family. Without Tee Ngiam, her brother would not have got a job, her sister, Annie, would not have gone to the university. Her mother had told her many times, "You have a good husband. Never do anything to displease him."

"Do I understand, Ngiam," she said, surprised at her own boldness, "that you don't wish me to re-marry after your death?"

"Why would you need to? You'll be the most amply provided for widow in Singapore." So it was not just a question of eight months or a year or three years. The man, from his grave, demanded life-time loyalty.

"Wait a minute," she said. "Why are we talking like this? Suppose I die before you?"

"If Patrick Chang could have foreseen his wife's behaviour tonight," said Tee Ngiam angrily, unable to let go of the subject of the widow's levity, "he would have turned in his coffin. His eyes would not have closed, but remained wide and staring."

The image was horrible; that night she had a dream in which she saw herself going to pay respects to the dead Patrick Chang in his coffin and retreating in horror at the sight of his large, open, staring eyes.

"Look, Ngiam," said Julie wearily, "let's stop all this weird talk. I could die before you. And you needn't mourn. You have my full permission to re-marry as soon as you wish. You are a very good husband and provider; I shouldn't deny any woman my good luck." She was not being sarcastic; she meant it.

"You haven't yet given me an answer," he said.

Their strange conversation that evening after the Chandras' party came back in all the uncanniness of its prescience when, a week later, she received an urgent call from her husband's office: he had collapsed and had been taken by ambulance to the hospital. She rushed over, but he was already dead of a massive heart attack. She sat down stunned, recollecting the conversation in its every detail. The sudden death, soon after the attempt to extract a promise from her, now shook the vaguely given promise into a firm commitment. The living man had asked; his corpse would receive a solemn undertaking from her. It would not be too late, for it is said that the newly dead see and hear everything that is going on.

Julie sat beside the corpse lying in the satin-lined, flower-bedecked coffin and spoke gently to it. "I'm sorry, Ngiam, if I gave you the impression that I wasn't grateful for all that you'd done for me and my family, that I was unwilling to grant your request." She made her commitment slowly, carefully, in the hearing of the family members. "Ngiam, I will be in the mourning black for you for three years." If the dead man needed that solace so badly, she would give it wholeheartedly. If his eyes opened now and his lips moved to say, "Not three years, but a lifetime," she would have said, "Anything you wish." No wife could go against the wishes of a dead husband who had been good to her.

At the wake, clad in deep black shirt and pants, she received visitors who came in a continuous stream, for her husband had been one of the most respected civil servants in Singapore. There was one visitor who puzzled her, for the woman, who was in her late thirties, was not only a total stranger, but wore full mourning black and was accompanied by five young children, also in mourning black. Ignoring everyone, the woman immediately went about the task of organising an orderly movement of the five children, beginning with the eldest, towards the corpse in the coffin, to pay their respects. When she looked up and saw Julie staring at her, she said matter-of-factly, "They're his children," and continued to supervise the exercise, carrying up the youngest child, a toddler, to look upon the dead man's face and blow him a kiss.

Julie was aware of something strange happening to her. She had split into two, one part observing the scene with the fascination of a calm onlooker and the other screaming in silent anguish and about to destroy itself in an explosion of shock, shame, rage and pure lust for revenge. The calm half, remembering that not once in the twenty five years of their marriage had they been a day apart, went up to the woman and asked, almost politely, "Just how did he do it?" And the woman, as if expecting the question, replied, just as politely, "Every Monday and Thursday afternoon." It came rushing in upon her with the impact of a hurricane or an earthquake, so that she stumbled and had to steady herself: the massive lie about having to lunch with the boss twice weekly, maintained over so many years. The shock of the lie destroyed all calmness; now she was pure fury, screaming so loudly that her sister and a friend rushed up to hold her. She heard herself screaming, "Liar! Liar!" and the woman, still carrying the toddler and not at all comprehending, said curtly, "I can give you all the proof you want." She had actually brought the proof – five photographs, one of each child, taken at birth, with the father proudly smiling. He was a good provider for that family too.

"Julie please –" said Annie holding her tightly, for she was still screaming. She broke free, ran into her room and locked herself in.

A hush fell upon everyone in the room; the shock had not fully sunk in. Later, for days, weeks, everyone would be talking, in hushed voices, of the secret life of Yeo Tee Ngiam, top civil servant, exemplary husband, who fathered a brood of children during his lunch breaks. But now, all awe and titillation had to be suspended in deference to the poor widow.

Nobody looked at the dead man, everybody looked at the door behind which the living widow had locked herself in.

After about half an hour, Annie knocked gently and called, "Julie, Julie, are you all right? Julie, please come out." They heard odd sounds coming from inside the room, of cupboards and drawers being opened and slammed shut.

Then the door opened. The alarms of the day surely culminated with this one, of the sight of Julie standing at the doorway in a red, slinky dress. She stood with studied insouciance, challenging everybody with her eyes. There was a ridiculous-looking red flower in her hair. The defiance of red was also in her high-heeled shoes, an evening purse, and in the lipstick and rouge, applied with such maniacal energy as to create a carnival caricature, a character right out of a burlesque. In a sea of decorous mourning colours of black, white, grey and blue, Julie's red stood out in shrieking revolt.

Somebody gasped; otherwise there was perfect stillness and silence. Everyone watched intently as Julie briskly strode up to the corpse in the coffin and began talking to it. It was still newly dead, and should be able to hear her. "I was going to throw it away," she said, her voice trembling in a dangerously rising fever of savage triumph, "but I'm glad I didn't, Ngiam. And I was going to throw this away, too," she continued, waving a postcard bearing a U.K. stamp, in front of the corpse's face, "but I think now I'll give Ron a reply!"

She adjusted the sequinned straps of the red dress, looked again at the dead corpse and suddenly began shouting in jubilation, "That's right, Ngiam! That's exactly what I want! Now you can look all you want! Go ahead, look all you want!"

The mistress rushed up crying, "Let me! Let me!", meaning that she too had seen the dead man's eyes suddenly open, and wanted to be the one to stroke the eyelids gently and lovingly, as that is the only way to close a dead man's staring eyes.

Some of the visitors had also witnessed the happening; they would later confirm with one another, and talk about it endlessly, in hushed tones.

"You get out of my husband's way," said Julie fiercely, pushing the mistress away roughly. "He wants to look at me like this; you leave him to do it."

Eight months. A year. Three years. She would wear that colour of her solace for much, much longer.

Adonis

Samuel was one of those rare males who combine astonishing good looks with a devotion to the scholarly and intellectual life. It was not just good looks that made the combination unusual; it was the vanity surrounding them. A young and handsome but untidy academic heedless of the unsightly stubble or crumpled shirt would not provoke any surprise; a handsome, meticulously groomed young professional who, in the midst of an absorbing study of Shakespeare or Sartre or Kuhn, studies his face in the mirror for blemishes, most certainly would.

The vanity came only later in his life. I was his classmate in St. Peter's Junior College and remember that in those days, he was already good-looking, with his fine features, robust, tall frame, and ready, bright smile. We were active members of the Literary and Drama Society and the fact that the plum role of handsome tragic hero for any school performance invariably went to him, could so easily have gone to his head and made him vain about his looks (I, alas, never had the part of the beauteous heroine, only that of some insignificant serving maid or, dressed as a man and ferociously moustachioed, as some minor villain).

I think it was X.X. Men's wear that did the mischief. The company, well-known for its trendy sportswear for men, was looking around for a suitable model to appear in its local advertisements. Samuel was spotted while he was walking along Shenton Way – he had just graduated and had started work in a legal firm. His fresh open countenance, bright eyes, good skin, thick hair, radiant smile and impressive height, made him the perfect model. Amused and flattered, Samuel agreed to feature in the advertisements which appeared in the local newspapers and on cinema and TV screens. Suddenly, his face had become one of the most recognisable in Singapore. Suddenly, pretty girls walking along Orchard Road turned to give him a second, a third look, to smile invitingly. Samuel was dazzled. From that time onwards, he felt an overwhelming need to preserve his good looks, as if he could not let all those pretty girls down. His handsomeness had become a responsibility and a burden.

At the time, I was among his close friends, ex-classmates who had kept in touch over the years. There were six of us; we called ourselves the Sextet. All bright, ambitious young professionals, we strove to achieve the five C's that defined the successful Singaporean – Car, Condominium, Cash, Credit Card, Country Club membership – but we were also anxious to go beyond the purely material to something far nobler, more worthy of the human spirit,which we spoke of vaguely as "self-fulfilment" and "self-actualisation" and "individuation", having a fondness for impressive terms. For Samuel, the ultimate fulfilment, as he had many times confided in me, was to be able to retire early and devote himself to reading, writing, travelling.

Had I, plain-looking as I was, ever harboured any deep feelings for Samuel? I confess now to some secret wish that I could never have been openly articulated, either because I did not want to acknowledge it myself, or, acknowledging it, knew it was hopeless and therefore best left hidden.

For the Sextet, comprising exactly three males and three females, all former classmates who had got along marvellously in school and who continued to meet as adults, had settled into that very comfortable state of genuine, open, innocent, fraternity and sorority known as Platonic love.

It was impossible that any romantic attachment would develop between any pair in the group. Samuel, Clarence and Bala on one side and Mabel, Hsuei Fong and myself on the other – we all came together in a happy, friendly, rambunctious way, meeting in one another's houses, going out together for meals or drinks, even going on holidays abroad together. If it is true that romance needs mystique, then romance was out for any pair in the Sextet, for there could be no mystique if you had gone to class every day in the same school uniform, agonised over the same homework, seen one another wince in the agony of a poor exam grade or a teacher's sharp reprimand.

One of the Sextet, Clarence Foo, paired up with a pretty young teacher in a secondary school and hence could spare little time for the group. But he tried his best to make it for every birthday celebration, that being the strongest tradition in the group. It was understood that with the years, more would find outside partners and drift away. But while we remained unattached, we were determined to keep the strong bonds of friendship that all acknowledged to have brought so much joy and comfort to our personal lives.

Samuel said to me, "Ariadne (that was his nickname for me), I know we will always be friends."

I do not know whether that statement, made like a promise, gave me more pain or pleasure. On the one hand, I was pleased by the loyalty of one so attractive and companionable. On the other hand, I was dismayed by a possible underlying meaning: that because of my plainness of looks, this strikingly handsome, vain man could never be attracted enough to go beyond friendship but would be too generous to pain me by relinquishing the friendship, even after, as seemed inevitable, he found a beautiful partner and drifted out of the group.

I dreaded the day.

I knew Samuel casually dated a whole range of pretty women. At one time, he almost got serious with an air stewardess, and at another time with a company secretary, both stunningly attractive women, the kind whose faces and figures would appear on the covers of glossy magazines. I knew Samuel was looking for a woman who combined beauty and brains. Beauty by itself would bore him immeasurably after a while, as his need for intellectual stimulation even in romantic settings was very great indeed. Once, as he told me, he took an extremely beautiful woman for dinner, and was aghast to find out that she was incapable of talking about anything apart from a pet Siamese cat and some perceived insult from a girlfriend. Samuel was looking for a woman endowed with both intellectual and physical attributes, to mirror his own endowments. I could only meet half that requirement. Without being unprepossessing, I was no Venus to team up with Adonis.

"Adonis," said Samuel ruminatively. The he smiled. "I like the name. Thanks, Ariadne!"

He sometimes invited me out for a meal or a drink, coming to fetch me in his Alpha Romeo. Sitting together at one of the fashionable French bistros he favoured, we must have attracted curious attention by the marked contrast in our looks, me in clothes that look dowdy no matter what I do with them, him the gleaming exemplar of ultimate male grooming in clothes, hair, skin-care. If I was monochrome, he was vivid rainbow.

This contrast, together with an easy back-slapping bonhomie far removed from the amatory coyness, must have caused curious onlookers to conclude that we simply could not be a regular couple.

Sometimes I found myself wishing we could be a regular couple. But for now I was content to be just the preferred companion for the intellectual sparring he enjoyed. We shared a love for books, discussion, argument, a free roaming intellectual curiosity that could cover amoeba, Existentialism and Papal Infallibility, all in the course of one quick bistro meal. His mind was always scintillating with ideas which he would call me to talk about. Once we talked about the nature of evil for hours on the phone. We also enjoyed trading favourite quotations from favourite philosophers, usually on the daunting subjects of life and death. My favourite was Socrates' defiant declaration that 'the unquestioned life is not worth living'; Samuel's was Anatole France's wry, crisp summary of the entirety of human history in one sentence: 'They were born, they suffered, they died.' That is, until he read something from Marcus Aurelius and excitedly phoned me about it: "'Today a drop of semen, tomorrow, a handful of ashes.'"

It became my favourite quotation too. The sheer violence of the imagery appealed to our sense of melodrama: the startling antithesis of stirring liquid life at one end and the sterile dust of death and negation at the other; the shocking reduction of the human body, in its fullness of size and solidity, to a tiny bit of spatial insignificance. Every time we attended a cremation and watched the large coffin enter the incinerator to emerge as a little urn of ashes, we thought of Marcus Aurelius.

Samuel said, "Sure, it will be today a drop of semen, tomorrow a handful of ashes, but what a lot of living in between!" He loved life, enjoying his work, his friends, his popularity, his books. He took meticulous care of his health, avoiding rich food, jogging every evening, doing work-outs in the gym a few times a week.

It was as if the handsome face and figure in the X.X. Men's Wear advertisement had to be preserved at all costs.

Once at a gathering of the Sextet, he made everyone promise that at his death we would make sure to remind his family not to leave the coffin open. "I want to be remembered as the live Sam, not the cold dead Sam," he said. It was part of a rather engaging, child-like self-centeredness that made him constantly refer to himself by name. "Samuel Lee Ern Hooi was beautiful in life. He was beautiful in death. This is how I want people to remember me always." And he showed us his favourite picture of himself, standing under a palm on a beach, the sunshine in his laughing eyes, the wind in his hair, as handsome as any movie star.

Once he visited a friend who was dying of cancer. The shock of seeing an emaciated, devastated body that had once been the most attractive and vibrant, reinforced his horror of leaving behind a last, ugly image in the minds of surviving friends, family, lovers.

"Nobody must ever see me like that," he murmured as he stumbled out of the hospital room, meaning that should he suffer the same misfortune as poor Woon Teng, he would either kill himself, or failing to do that, instruct his family to turn away all visitors.

In February 1991, just a week before we were due to celebrate his thirty-third birthday for him at a special surprise party that we knew he would enjoy, Samuel died in a car accident in New Zealand. It was a horrible accident, in which the car he was in with somebody was crushed by a truck. Samuel was almost decapitated. My first feeling, on receiving the news, was, curiously, one of great relief: "Thank God for the death." Permanent disfigurement or reduction to a vegetative state would have been crueller for Samuel.

Getting together to talk in hushed tones about the terrible tragedy and to comfort his bereaved family, we recollected that Samuel had once said he thought it no bad thing to die young, like the romantic poet Keats, and be forever frozen in a permanence of youth and beauty. We told Samuel's family members about his favourite photograph which they promptly enlarged and framed, to be used for his funeral, and also for the obituary in the newspaper. Samuel Lee Ern Hooi, aged thirty-two, would be remembered, down the years, in the radiance of his youthful good looks, while we would all grow old and gray and feeble. The mangled corpse, lying in the mortuary in a New Zealand hospital, had been quickly identified by a relative who had gone in place of Samuel's poor distraught parents, and had been quickly put in a coffin to be taken home. Back in Singapore, as the coffin stood in the funeral parlour, its lid remained resolutely shut, in deference to Samuel's wish.

The trauma for me began when we denied Samuel this wish.

Actually, it was Mabel who started it all. Now I wonder if like me, she had nursed deep, secret feelings for Samuel. She was the most inconsolable among us as we sat together in the funeral parlour through the three nights of the wake. On the last night, before the funeral in the morning, Mabel made an urgent request: she wanted to place her birthday gift for Samuel – she said it was a very special gift – in the coffin, beside the corpse, and she suggested that, in the late hours of the night, when everybody had left the parlour, we, his closest and dearest friends, should open the coffin for this last farewell of gifts.

The suggestion, so terrifying at first, began to work on us, assuming a strange, irresistible appeal: we each had bought a gift for Sam, selected with great care, in preparation for the birthday party (I had taken the trouble, through a friend in New York, to get a rare edition of a book of Yeats' poems, which I knew Sam had wanted very much), and had looked forward to seeing the glow of pleasure that invariably greeted each gift. It would be a fitting farewell from loved friends. At the back of our minds was the unspoken question: could we bare to look upon the face of his corpse?

Mabel's wish prevailed. In the stillness of night, by ourselves in the funeral parlour, we lifted the coffin lid and put in the birthday gifts. Mabel was weeping silently. The rest of us were dry-eyed.

I cannot bear to describe what I saw, except to say, very briefly, that I wished, as soon as I looked at the face, I had not agreed to the decision. Suffice it to say that it was the most terrifying sight in the world for me, made more terrifying by the fact of the near decapitation and the mortician's shoddy efforts at restoration. Samuel Lee Ern Hooi, handsome young man, with the movie-star looks, had been transformed, by a most cruel death, into the most appalling sight.

For days, weeks, months, the horrible image haunted me. I tried desperately to erase it by superimposing upon it the remembered image of Samuel alive, of Samuel laughing in sunshine and breeze in the favourite photograph. All to no avail.

One night I woke up screaming from a dream. I was in the funeral parlour looking upon the dead body of Samuel in the coffin. It was a young, handsome, whole Samuel. Then I saw the handsome face distort before my eyes, swell into the horribly bloated, bruised, discoloured face I had seen that secret night of our daring deed in the funeral parlour, saw one half of a jaw crack open to become a gaping cavern of blood and broken bone, saw one eye dissolving in a mess of blood and torn tissue. I saw the head slip from the broken neck, saw the horrendous result of the careless mortician's work that had not ensured a proper re-attachment. It was when I heard Samuel say from his coffin, in a clear voice, "Ariadne, I will not forgive you for doing this to me," that I woke up panting, bathed in sweat.

None of the others had had any dreams of Samuel or heard any words of reproach. Why had I been singled out? It did not seem fair. Whatever the reason, I would seek Samuel's forgiveness at once and alone.

When alive, Samuel had practiced some kind of religious eclecticism, going to midnight mass every Christmas eve in a Catholic church, accepting an invitation to speak at a Bahai gathering, joining in some Buddhist cleansing ritual, visiting a Hindu temple. I went to all the churches and temples I had known him to visit, sitting quietly in a corner as he had done, and saying to him from my heart, "Sam, if you happen to be here now, please let me know you have forgiven me." Could one soothe the mortified feelings of a vain ghost by assuring it that one would always remember its beauty? I tried. "Sam, I will always remember you as you have always been to us – Adonis."

Samuel was clearly not appeased. There was another dream. This time he sat up in his coffin and thrust his shattered, monstrous face into mine. "You want to remember me like this?"

I did not mention my dreams to any of the others. The ardent Mabel had gone into a year of self-imposed mourning. She had Samuel's photograph set in a beautiful silver frame and placed on a bedside table. She said she could feel Sam's presence on certain nights, giving her a sense of ineffable peace. I envied Mabel.

In my desperation to make peace with Samuel, I did something I would never have thought possible. I consulted a medium who was supposed to be able to contact the dead, take messages to them, convey messages from them, speak on their behalf. He was a middle-aged man, dressed in white, speaking in a low, sepulchral voice. I was totally unimpressed, indeed impatient with his vague generalisations and deliberately undecipherable utterances. Then I heard about a much acclaimed psychic from Australia who was on a visit to Singapore; she was supposed to be able to look back into the past, interpret the present, predict the future with astonishing accuracy, as well as communicate with the dead. It was a very expensive consultation and once again I left unimpressed by what I thought was a great deal of psychobabble and gobbledygook. Both the medium and the psychic had described Samuel's spirit as being troubled and confined to some grey, misty area. But it was slowly making its way into a region of soft radiant sunshine, peace and joy, guided by his friends' prayers and love for him. Soon the grey mists now enveloping him would evaporate.

I didn't pay a few hundred dollars to hear about troubled spirits, grey mists and radiant sunshine. I wanted to hear Samuel's voice, recognise his mannerisms of speech, react to a specific message, whether of forgiveness or continuing displeasure. I wanted some real proof.

One morning, about six months after Samuel's death, I had a call from one of his family members. While going through his possessions, they had found a little piece of paper, with an address written on it, in between the pages of a memo pad on which Samuel used to write down every night the things he was supposed to do the following day. (Samuel was a very systematic and organised person, always making checklists like that.) Since the piece of paper bore my name, he must have intended it for me. Would I go to pick it up?

I hurried over breathlessly, in a mixture of excitement, puzzlement and trepidation. An address? Of whom? Was it someone that Samuel had wanted me to meet? Something he had wanted me to do for him as a favour? A sudden thought struck me. Could it be a message from beyond, and could it be Samuel's answer to my anguished pleas for forgiveness and an end to those horrible dreams?

It had an address that was totally unfamiliar, of a flat in an HDB block of flats in an old district in Singapore. There was no telephone number with the address, but the initials 'E.V.' scribbled in the corner of the piece of paper, with a small question mark over it. 'E.V.'? Was it the name of the person residing at the given address? Who was he/she? Or was it a mere random scribbling, unrelated to the address?

Then I remembered something. One evening over coffee – it must have been at least a year before the accident – Samuel and I were talking about spiritualism, mediumistic trances, spirit writing, the entire range of paranormal phenomena. When I expressed interest in going to a spiritualist just for experience, Samuel suddenly remembered a friend telling him abut a certain woman medium in Singapore, one of the best, who had impressed many of her clients by giving detailed descriptions of their deceased ones, and conveying information which at the time seemed puzzling but later proved amazingly accurate. E.V. – I remembered Samuel had mentioned an Evelyn Voon or Emmelyn Voon, a woman of mixed Chinese, Thai and Dutch parentage, who clearly had remarkable powers.

I lost no time in contacting E.V.

As had happened on that awful night when we opened the coffin and peered into Sam's face, I regretted, with all my heart and continue to regret to this day, the decision to track down the address on the piece of paper found after Sam's death, and handed over to me as if Sam wanted me to lift the veil of death's mystery and peer into his face in the shadowed realm of his new abode.

I found the address easily. It was a small flat on the sixth floor of a drab block of flat that would soon be pulled down to make way for a gleaming condominium. E.V. – Mrs Emmelyn, not Evelyn, Voon – was very old, white-haired, frail-looking woman with pale skin and light brown eyes. I had eerie feeling, as she opened the door and silently led me to a small sparsely furnished, darkened room at the back, that she had been expecting me.

I had only wanted to use Mrs. Emmelyn Voon's mediumistic powers to say sorry to Samuel, to avow everlasting affection and to hear from him what he wanted me to do by way of more expiation for my act of gross insensitivity. I got much more than I had bargained for. Mrs. Voon went into a gentle trance; her head dropped over her chest, her eyes closed. She seemed to be drifting into sleep when suddenly she began to speak. *It was the distinct voice of Samuel.* Samuel's slight lisp, his habit of rolling his r's, the staccato whenever he got carried away in an argument – all these came through Mrs. Emmelyn Voon's slightly open mouth, as she lay slumped in her chair. I couldn't believe my ears.

"Sam, please forgive me."

"There's nothing to forgive."

"Sam, I love you."

"Adonis loves you too."

"Sam, is there anything you want me to do?"

"Nothing, Ariadne."

Adonis, Ariadne. The proofs I needed, coming in quick succession, were truly amazing. I wish it had ended at this point. Then there would have been no regret of the visit, no troubling puzzlement that continues to this day.

I was staring at Mrs. Voon. Slowly, her features were changing before my eyes, melting, then re-configuring, as in a horror movie. *She was taking on the appearance of Sam's face in the coffin.* I saw the bloated, discoloured face, the shattered jaw, the head almost falling off the neck.

In my shock, I must have blacked out for a few minutes. When I opened my eyes again, I saw Mrs. Voon looking silently at me, her old frail face even paler, her light brown eyes tinged with a gentle melancholy.

When I got up to leave, I stammered, in the hope of a confirmation from Mrs. Voon, "My imagination played tricks on me just now. I saw your face change into my dead friend's."

Mrs. Voon said, "It wasn't your imagination," and showed me to the door. She died two weeks later.

I don't understand the logic of it all. Sam had, with those frightful dreams, punished me but not any of the Sextet who were equally culpable in that sacrilegious act on the last night of the wake. Yet it was really less an act of sacrilege than of love, and Sam would have been the first to realise this. The dear friend who in life had shown warm appreciation for gifts selected with great thoughtfulness and care, had in death punished me for wanting to place in his coffin a gift I had selected with the greatest care of all. Sam, through Mrs. Voon, had told me he had forgiven me, had indeed reciprocated my professions of affectionate regard, yet had chosen, through the same Mrs. Voon, to reinforce the image he had never wanted me to see in the first place.

It is all very bewildering. I don't understand the logic of it all. Perhaps in that mysterious world of the dead that Sam has gone to, in the howling silence he is now part of, the normal rules of our logic don't apply.

A drop of semen, a handful of ashes. Beyond that, is the mystery even bleaker and sadder?

The Gift

My cousin Joon Hong, who is a marketing executive, sees ghosts. At least, he claims to. I believe him. Because it is a claim never made with bravado but with great reluctance, even a little resentment. Also because I have seen him, when we are out together, stare at something, give a little start, then quickly give me a sideways glance, as if to ascertain that I have been spared the startling vision. Joon Hong is thirteen years my senior, and has taken the role of a protector and mentor. He says his experiences with the world of the supernatural are not exactly pleasant ones, and does not wish me to share them. I ask him to tell me about them. Sometimes he is willing, at other times extremely reluctant, as if the telling would result in harm to himself or me.

Once we were walking past the void deck of a block of HDB flats in Ang Keng Road, on our way to visit a friend in a neighbouring block. A wake was being held on the deck. From where we were, we could see the upper half of the face of the dead man as he lay in his coffin, surrounded by wreaths of orchids and chrysanthemums mounted on wooden stands, and tall, flower-bedecked crosses which, together with a large crucifix hanging on the wall behind the coffin, pointed to the dead man's Christian faith. His large framed photo was set on a small table at the foot of the coffin and was flanked by white candles. It showed a middle-aged man with thinning hair and heavy black-rimmed glasses, a man who is immediately identifiable as a civil servant or business executive. Facing the coffin were rows of chairs which were already beginning to be occupied by visitors in sober shades of black, grey and blue, in preparation for some ceremony about to be conducted by a white-robed priest seen talking to one of the visitors. A tired-looking middle-aged woman in a white blouse and black skirt, presumably the widow, was receiving a stream of visitors, accepting their condolences and donations with a brave, weak smile.

We saw all of this as we walked past. I noticed Joon Hong pause suddenly to stare at something. I followed his gaze which was fixed on a spot to the right of the coffin. I watched Joon Hong watch whatever it was for a full minute. Later he told me it was the ghost of the dead man. The ghost looked much older than the man in the photograph; his hair was much thinner, his face more gaunt. He was wearing not the formal suit and tie of the corpse laid out in the coffin, but maroon cotton pyjamas with some kind of white or greyish embroidery on the upper shirt pocket.

"If I go up and asked the widow what he was wearing when he died," said Joon Hong, "I'm sure she'll give exactly this description."

"Will you?"

"Never! Are you mad? Always let ghosts alone. The dead and their survivors – leave them alone."

"What was the ghost doing?" I wanted to know.

"Nothing much," said Joon Hong. "Just looking at the visitors with a mixture of mild curiosity and puzzlement. Maybe he doesn't even realise he's dead."

"Were you scared?"

Joon Hong has seen too many ghosts to be scared. But there was one ghost that terrified him. He seldom has nightmares about the ghosts he encounters, but this one rampaged through his dreams for three successive nights.

He was on a golf course with his friends, enjoying a much deserved respite from the increasing pressures of work as a result of a new promotion, when he suddenly felt someone staring at him and turned round sharply to see a woman under some trees, a short distance away. She looked dishevelled; her clothes were torn and her long hair, which was wet, was plastered in strands on her face, neck and shoulders. Her eyes were wide open with terror; so was her mouth, opening and shutting in some desperate wordless communication. She moved slightly under the trees, and it was then that Joon Hong saw, to his shock, that the wetness of her long hair was the wetness of blood.

The ghastly apparition lasted only a few seconds. Joon Hong told me he could not continue playing after that, but stumbled away in a daze, to the astonishment of his friends, making straight for the clubhouse to get a drink to steady his nerves. He later found out that in 1985, a woman had been murdered and her body found in exactly that spot under the tree. The poor woman had been raped and her throat brutally slit.

Joon Hong vaguely remembered reading a report in the Straits Times, when he was still an undergraduate, about a naked mutilated body of a young woman found dumped in some undergrowth near Serenity Hill, which was later developed as a golf course. He took trouble to go to the offices of the Straits Times to look up that back copy, nearly fifteen years ago, and managed to find the report. The woman was a Theresa Mah, aged twenty-eight, who had held a number of jobs, including that of bar waitress. Her murderer was never found. The photo accompanying the report matched the apparition, in every detail.

"Was she the most frightening ghost you've ever seen?"

Joon Hong will not tell me about his most frightening experience which involved an old woman, a caretaker in a temple, who went mad one day, then hanged herself from a tree in the temple grounds.

"That was thirty years ago, but she's still around," says Joon Hong with a shudder.

"Tell me," I persist. But Joon Hong shakes his head. He is being protective. He knows I have a fervid imagination that will make me experience his encounters vicariously and populate my dreams with his ghosts.

"No way," he says.

"It's a gift," I say with real envy. "To be able to see things that other people can't must be a gift. Makes life more interesting."

My closest brush with the supernatural was hearing some strange, ghostly wails one night when my classmates and I were camping on St. John's Island, which I later discovered to be a clever hoax perpetrated by a rival group of campers determined to oust us from the best camping spot on the island.

"I would like to see a ghost. A *real* ghost," I say wistfully, "I wish I had your gift, Hong."

"I was ill for a week after that encounter on the golf course," says Hong. "A gift? I'd say to whoever gave it to me, 'Please take it back.'"

Tribute

At the height of his prosperity – he had just opened the *tenth* Chwee Neo Roast Duck Eating House – Tan Tua Bah wept. At the precise fulfilment of the fortune-teller's dazzling prediction that he would one day own a house bigger than any that those rich neighbours and relatives who had looked down on his family could ever dream of – he had just acquired a six-million-dollar bungalow in Chester Park, which he was presently renovating to rent to the American ambassador to Singapore – Tan Tua Bah felt a sadness in his heart.

The sadness was on account of his mother who had died more than fifty years ago, at age thirty-four, when he was only a small boy. Hers was the classic story of the courage and endurance of a young widow, with no education or resources other than fierce determination to bring up her children and see them succeed in the world. This, together with a sturdiness of constitution inherited from peasant ancestors way back in China, enabled Chwee Neo to go through those cruel years.

They were years of unremitting toil. She would get up at four every morning – "even before cock-crow," she used to joke – and worked till midnight, cleaning, cooking, washing, mending at home and going to the town some distance from her small *kampung* to do, for a pittance, odd jobs such as grating coconut, chopping firewood, slaughtering fowl for wedding or temple celebrations, in order to scrape together enough food to feed her four sons, clothe them and see them through school. Poor Chwee Neo's overworked body gave way at last. Even when ill with some strange illness that was eating up her liver and other internal organs, according to an old relative, she struggled to keep the family going.

The mere mention of his mother brought tears to Tua Bah's eyes. The bitterest regret in his life was that she never lived to enjoy the good life that his three brothers and especially himself would have so joyfully given her. He was the most successful of them all, though the least educated, having left school at Primary Three. The thought that one of his brothers, who actually went to college, could never have a fraction of his wealth gave him an immense secret satisfaction. During the Chinese New Year, Uncle Tua Bah's *ang pows* were always the biggest, at least one hundred dollars, compared to their ten or five, so that his nephews and nieces never failed to visit him on the first day of the New Year itself.

There had been an article in the Straits Times on those Singaporeans who had been born into stark poverty but made good in a spectacular way. He was one of just a handful identified by the newspaper and had been interviewed at length by the reporter, an enthusiastic young lady named Amanda Goh. In his best shirt, wearing one of his three Rolex watches and an enormous lucky jade ring that he had bought in Hong Kong for ten thousand dollars, Tua Bah was posed by Miss Goh for a photograph beside his tenth and newest Roast Duck Eating House. He had been particularly pleased that the reporter had made much of his grateful naming of every single one of the eating houses after his dead mother. He was a little upset, though, that she had under-reported the amount spent on the major renovation of a row of four old shophouses to make his latest eating house the best and largest in Singapore, but was too polite to call her and request a correction of the inaccuracy.

Now the Feast of the Hungry Ghosts was coming round again, when Tua Bah's grateful love brimmed over and he personally supervised the cleaning of his mother's tomb at the Kek Lok Cemetery and the offering of the best food and tea to her ghost, which, like the others during this auspicious season, would be returning to this world to receive the tributes of sons and daughters and grandchildren. At the peak of his prosperity and in the tenderest of filial dispositions, Tua Bah racked his brains to think of a tribute truly worthy of his mother's selfless devotion. She had had all the suckling pig, steamed chicken, braised duck, fried noodles and fragrant oranges and pomelos that she could eat. He had never stinted on his offerings, always insisting on the best, down to the last joss-stick (from Taiwan) to stick in the urn on her altar, the last candle (from U.K., since he believed that Western candles were superior to Asian ones) to burn in front of her photograph.

What would be te ultimate tribute?

Tua Bah had an idea, and the more he thought about it, the more excited he got. A house – that was what he would give her as the climax to the offerings over the years. Not one of those usual ghost houses that could be so easily obtained from the makers in Pagoda Street or Chin Choo Street, probably made from cheap paper. A special one, made from the finest materials. A really magnificent one, unstoppable in size, beauty, cost. Tua Bah consulted with the makers of the ghost houses and discovered, to his dismay, that none of them felt equal to the task of constructing the house he had in mind. He showed them a picture of the enormous, awesome ghost-house, almost as big as a regular house, which he had cut out of a magazine from Taiwan. It must have used up an incalculable amount of paper, wire, bamboo slats, silk cloth, beads, gold and silver paint.

"We can't do it; only the Taiwanese experts can do anything like that," they said, shaking their heads.

"Then I'll fly in the Taiwanese experts," said Tua Bah.

And he did just that. He let his plans be known to the reporter Amanda Goh, who once again came over eagerly, sensing a truly captivating story.

"Twenty five thousand dollars!" she gasped. Tua Bah wanted to say that was just a conservative estimate, but modestly refrained.

As the expert craftsmen worked on the house which, because of its size, would take longer than the usual ten minutes or so to burn down to ashes, Tua Bah went on a rampage of information-seeking concerning his mother. He wanted family and elderly relatives to tell him what they could remember of his mother's favourite food, drink, clothes, furniture, cooking utensils, crockery, etc., of any wish she might have inadvertently let drop, for this or that luxury, for instance, a special food too expensive to buy, a blouse or an item of jewellery she had seen on someone else and yearned for. He listened intently to every recollection, stored up every detail, and then went to the craftsmen, to convert his mother's dream into reality. His oldest brother remembered that their mother once spoke longingly of sleeping on a soft cotton mattress instead of an old mat. Tua Bah instantly instructed the craftsmen to make ten paper mattresses. An old relative told him that his mother once went to pawn the only remaining possession of worth she had – her two gold teeth. Tua Bah immediately instructed the craftsmen to make two sets of gold teeth, which they did, after much persuasion, in the finest, most exquisite gold paper.

There was one more thing that Tua Bah wanted to give his mother. He had been told that she could have been saved from her early cruel death if she had had the money to buy the necessary medicine. What was her illness? What medicine did she need? Could the dead be comforted by medicine that they had been too poor to buy when alive? Tua Bah was determined to include a huge supply of it in the ghost house. He did not know if pills or tablets and liquid mixtures could be simulated in paper, but he would pay the craftsmen to do it.

Then an old relative suddenly recollected something which made Tua Bah weep afresh. His mother had a secret. For years, as she struggled to bring up her children, she allowed herself a small luxury which she was too embarrassed to let her sons know about. Or perhaps she felt too guilty about it, because it involved spending money on herself. Every evening, when the children were asleep, she would help herself to a drink, a cheap *samsu* made and sold illicitly in the village shops. It gave her wracked body a few moments of ease and her troubled mind, always worrying about the next meal or the next school fees, a few moments of solace. Best of all, the potent brew allowed her to have a few hours of precious sleep before the next day's round of toil and sorrow. It was this cheap toxic brew, said the old relative, that had rapidly destroyed her liver.

Tua Bah went in great haste to the craftsmen to make a final request for cases of paper Hennessey brandy. The craftsmen were getting a little impatient with the constant requests for this or that addition to an already well-stocked ghost-house. Tua

Beh kept telling them that money was no problem; his mother simply had to have the best.

"Let this be the last request," they said testily.

The ghost-house was soon ready. It was breathtaking in its size and accoutrements, being almost as big as a real house, with a handsome pagoda roof of red and gold tiles, enormous pillars around which twined magnificent dragons with silver scales, an entrance guarded by two lions in gold and purple, rooms with tasselled curtains and exquisite furniture more beautiful than the intricately carved chairs, tables and beds they represented, sets of fine eating and drinking utensils, wardrobes of rich silk blouses, trousers and robes, boxes of jade, silver, gold and diamond ornaments. Outside the mansion stood three cars – a Rolls Royce, a Chevrolet and a Mercedes – and two rickshaws. An impressive retinue of paper servants stood ready to do the bidding of the mistress of this imposing mansion.

The young reporter Amanda Goh was excitedly taking notes, and the photographer she had brought along was busy taking pictures. Just when they thought the house was ready to be ceremonially consigned to the flames by two temple priests at the ready, they heard a shout and a screech of brakes and saw Tua Bah jumping out of a van and giving instructions to the van driver and an assistant to carry out something from the vehicle. It was case after case of XO, two dozen cases in all, the reporter counted in astonishment, which Tua Bah, now flushed with pride and excitement, instructed the men to put inside the ghost-house. Paper brandy as well as *real* brandy, the best, the most expensive, such as even the most affluent denizen of that other world would never have the luxury of tasting.

Extremely impressed by such a brilliant show of filial piety, Amanda Goh faithfully reported its cost. "Thirty thousand dollars," she gushed. "Mr Tan Tua Bah, of the famous chain of Chwee Neo Roast Duck Eating Houses, specially brought in craftsmen from Taiwan to make this indescribably beautiful paper ghost-house for his mother Madam Lau Chwee Neo, who died half a century ago. He said it was his way of honouring a most beloved parent."

Tua Bah was pleased with the report but was once more rather upset by Miss Goh's failure to get her facts totally correct. He had stipulated the actual amount spent as forty thousand, not thirty thousand, the additional amount being the cost of the very expensive XO. But once again, he was too modest and courteous to call her to request the correction.

Alien

I am an engineer from Madras, India, with the status of Permanent Resident in Singapore. I came to work in Singapore some years ago, enticed by what I had heard of the city-state's cleanliness, orderliness and ambitious commitment to the goal of front position among the world's most technologically advanced, successful, prosperous and gracious societies in the twenty-first century.

It is also one of the most superstitious societies in the world. I have never met people who so enthusiastically (though discreetly) consult fortune-tellers and believe in ghosts and evil spirits, as Singaporeans. It is thanks to this belief that I, an alien, can afford to own an apartment in this unique country, part of whose uniqueness must be the astronomical price of property. One can spend one's entire life paying off the loan for a tiny, three-room apartment. When I tell my friends back home in India how much I have paid for my little flat on the fourteenth floor of a block that is one of six closely packed together in one of numerous such housing estates in Singapore, their jaws drop and they gasp "But you can get a mansion here with that kind of money!" As I said, it is thanks to Singaporean ghosts that my wife Kamala and I, with our little boy Ravi, are comfortably, happily settled in a place of our own in Singapore.

It all began with a small advertisement, one of hundreds, in the 'Houses/Flats for Sale/Rent' page in the Straits Times. I yelped with joy, circling it with a bright red pencil. At last. A flat that suited both my requirements concerning location and size, and my very modest budget. I called the advertiser and owner, Mr. Yap. He made arrangements for me to view the place. He was a thin, middle-aged, nervous-looking man. He said if I were a genuine buyer, I should make an offer quickly, as there were many interested buyers.

One of the first things Kamala and I had learnt when we first came to Singapore was that Singaporeans love the act of bargaining. Nothing gives Singaporeans greater satisfaction than the feeling that they have succeeded in knocking a substantial amount off the original asking price – whether of fish, shoes, car or property – no matter that the price had been impossibly jacked up in the first place in readiness for the knocking off. Indeed, Singaporeans have raised the act of bargaining to the status of a complex social ritual, giving pleasure to both sides.

So I coolly made Mr. Yap an offer that was so grossly below the asking price that I blushed inwardly. Waiting for the exhilarating process of bargaining to begin, I was astonished when Mr. Yap accepted my offer. "Okay," he said.

The flat was mine!

I phoned my good friend Boh Yuen in great excitement.

Boh Yuen and I work for the same engineering company. His immediate reaction was: "There's a catch somewhere. No property in Singapore goes that cheap. You'd better find out, Prem."

It was too late, but I decided to find out. The truth was so unnerving that I decided to keep it from Kamala.

The flat had once belonged to a relative of Mr. Yap. One night, many years ago, the man killed his entire family – his wife and three young sons – and then himself. It was the most systematically carried-out murder-cum-suicide, planned to the last detail and meticulously recorded, in advance, in a letter which the man wrote just before his death, addressed to no one in particular, and left on the table with a glass paperweight on it.

The man was clearly a stickler for factual accuracy, providing, in his letter, precise details of time, sequence of actions, motive. He had written, in his neat handwriting, very simply and matter-of-factly: "I, Jek Chai Mun, killed my three sons, Jek Wen Yong, Jek Wen Kee and Jek Wen Shin, between 11:30p.m. and 11:55 on 12 June 1980, with the help of my wife, Lily Lim Eng Siew. (The three boys aged eight, six and four were found strangled on a double bed.) At 12:05 I helped my wife to hang herself. (She was found suspended from the ceiling, her legs tied together. That must have been where the help was given.) At 12:35, I killed myself. (He was found hanging beside her.) I would like the proceeds of the sale of my flat to settle my debts (he had been a compulsive gambler, incurring enormous debts, and had also been suffering from ill health) and the balance to be donated to charity."

A close-up photograph of the letter had been included in a report in the Straits Times. The report emphasised the painstaking preparations that the couple had made for the family's gruesome tryst with death: all were dressed in their best clothes, the man in shirt and tie, the woman in neat *samfu* and a pearl necklace, the boys in neat shirts and pants (I wondered if the parents had cooked up an elaborate lie to the children, about going to a party or some big celebration?). There was an altar on which stood a framed formal picture of the family, with offerings of candles, tea and oranges set neatly before it. According to the report, the candles were still burning when the bodies were discovered. The Jek family massacre was probably the only instance in the annals of suicide in Singapore where scrupulous preparations had included paying advance respect to one's own dead self.

For days I was haunted, not so much by the horrifying image of three dead bodies on a bed and two hanging from the ceiling, as by the chilling gravity of the suicide note. What manner of a man could write a note like that, and then proceed to act on it?

"Now you know why the man was in such a hurry to sell the flat," said Boh Yuen unfeelingly. "It must have been vacant for years. Nobody would want to stay in such an unclean place. You're going to be visited by five ghosts, Prem."

"Well," I said, "I'd like to meet the man's ghost and give him a good ticking-off for dragging along his poor wife and three sons. Come to think of it, he deserves more than a ticking-off. A real good punch or two."

Once the initial horror was over, I thought no more of the tragedy, relegating Boh Yuen's five ghosts to that category of idle, worthless beliefs that ought not to be a part of the life of this modern, pragmatic, highly successful society. I immersed myself in the thrill of new ownership, renovating the flat, getting new furniture, watching Kamala energetically put up curtains, pictures, ornaments, setting up a special playroom for Ravi, with plenty of space for his numerous toys.

Then the sounds began.

Kamala said, "Prem, I think you should so something about the rats in the kitchen. Also, the neighbours. All those rapping and tapping sounds at night. A real nuisance."

I had heard the sounds. I didn't think they came from rats or neighbours. Once when I was sitting alone in the sitting room reading, I looked up and saw a picture on the wall opposite me begin to move. Then it crashed to the floor. On another occasion, on a perfectly still night, I saw the curtains of one of the windows flapping wildly, and felt a sudden draught of cold air sweep through the room luckily. Kamala was asleep.

I could live with the noises, but when the ghosts started showing themselves, I knew I had to do something. I am as rationalist as they come; part of the rationalism is a pragmatism that is ready to suspend all sceptical thinking to solve a problem. The ghosts of the Jek family were becoming a problem. An Indian would know nothing about appeasing Chinese ghosts. So I consulted Boh Yuen. He turned pale, put his hands to his ears and said, "Stop, I don't want to hear."

Boh Yuen, Chief Engineer, who would never authorise any digging or piling work or the chopping down of old trees without first discreetly getting a priest from a temple to conduct ceremonies of propitiation, refused to listen to my tales of the hauntings in my flat. He said, "They will give me bad dreams."

One day Kamala said to me, "Prem, there's something strange going on in this flat. Last night I was in Ravi's room, putting him to sleep, when I looked up. Guess what I saw? Three whitish shapes near the door. The shapes of three children, of different heights. When I looked again, they were gone. I swear I hadn't imagined it!"

Could Ravi's room have been the one where the three boys had been murdered? A few days later, Kamala said she was walking out of the bedroom the night before to get a drink of water from the kitchen when she again saw the three shapes. This time she saw them clearly.

"Little boys," she said, in an awe-stricken tone. "Three little boys, huddled together, looking scared. Somehow, I wasn't frightened."

To this day, Kamala does not know the truth about the tragedy.

One evening shortly after, as I was watching Ravi play with his toys in his room, I saw him suddenly look up and fix his eyes on a spot a short distance away. I followed the direction of his fascinated gaze, but saw nothing. Still looking on with wide, delighted eyes, Ravi smiled, gurgled and put out his hand. He is a gregarious toddler who invariably approaches other children with friendly gestures as soon as he sees them. I watched in growing unease as he got up from the floor and toddled towards the invisible presence. He stopped, still smiling and gurgling and waving his arms about in overtures of friendliness. Then, to my horror, I saw him stumble and fall backwards, as if some child had given him a sudden shove. Ravi sat on the floor and began to cry. I picked him up and fled from the room. Later, I made arrangements for my wife and son to stay with a relative, while I thought about how to deal with this new, disturbing development. To Kamala's protest, I simply said, "There's a problem, please do what I say."

Ghosts are tolerable, provided they do not harm. But when they get malignant, something must be done. The child ghosts in my flat were getting to be hostile. I had to protect my small son from them.

Boh Yuen got out of his timidity enough to provide the help I sought. I wanted to do whatever Chinese people do to get rid of the ghosts from their houses. Boh Yuen consulted a temple medium on my behalf. The medium said that the spirits of the dead man and his wife had "passed on", but those of the three sons were somehow still trapped in the flat and were presently suffering a great deal.

"That's most unfair," I complained on their behalf. "That dastardly father should be the one to suffer, not his innocent children." My concern was how to help these poor three spirits "pass on", whatever that was, as long as it ended their torment. I was prepared to take part in rituals of appeasement, like the offerings of huge feasts of delicious food, or the burning of huge stacks of ghost money, that I had seen and been fascinated by when I first came to Singapore. Would the offerings of an alien be accepted?

The temple medium said these would be of no use. The truth was that there was something in the flat that belonged to the boys that had to be returned to them, to free their spirits from their imprisonment on earth. As long as this something remained unreturned, their ghosts would wander about in confusion and misery.

One night, I actually heard the sounds of the children's sobbing. They were the anguished cries of impossibly burdened hearts. Almost mad with frustration, I said to Boh Yuen, "For heaven's sake, why can't your medium tell us what this something is, so that we can look for it and return it immediately?" My imagination, very fertile at times, simply could not figure out what this mysterious possession was. Clothes? Toys? School books? The bed on which they died? We had made sure to clear out everything when we moved in. Or perhaps it was something non-material, non-tangible?

I pressed Boh Yuen to go to another medium who might be more adept at interpreting the wishes of the dead. This medium was equally unhelpful. What a frustratingly complex culture I had unwittingly wandered into.

One evening, I suddenly had an idea. I decided to appeal

to the ghosts directly. I spoke aloud, in English which I hoped they would understand; after all, it is the working language in Singapore and the language of communication among its diverse ethnic groups. Besides, communication between ghosts and humans supposedly transcends language and culture. So I, an Indian, spoke in English to three little Chinese ghosts. I spoke slowly, expressing my feelings of frustration and concern simply and honestly. Above all, I begged the ghosts to lead me, whenever they were ready, to that something still present in the flat, whatever it was, so that I could return it to them, however they wished it to be done. I ended by saying that there was nothing which would make me happier than to be instrumental in freeing them from their sad captivity on earth and releasing them to eternal peace and rest. (I almost wanted to add that if I were them I wouldn't care to go join that undeserving father.)

That night, as I lay in bed, I kept hoping to have a dream in which the three little Chinese ghosts would appear to me and give instuctions. I had heard that for the Chinese, the dream was one of the most effective conduits of information and advice from the other world. No luck. No dream.

The next night, I thought I heard noises and woke up. The noises stopped. I couldn't get back to sleep. Then something made me get up and make my way out of the room and into one at the back of the flat, which Kamala had been planning to convert into a study for me. I could feel myself being helplessly borne along on a tide of energy not my own. In the room, I made straight for a small table in a corner. It was an item of furniture that somehow we had forgotten to get rid off, together with the rest, when we moved in. There were two drawers; I opened one, put my hand inside and brought out a small bundle of something, wrapped in soft cloth. Till now, I was in darkness. I switched on the light and looked at what was in my hand. It was a neat bundle; the wrapping was a piece of faded pink satin. Slowly I removed the wrapping. Inside there were three identical small white paper packets, each containing something which my fingers, feeling gently through the paper, could not identify. Then I noticed that on each packet was written, neatly, a name. The names of the three boys with what must be their dates of birth. Jek Wen Yong, 14/2/72, Jek Wen Kee, 12/6/74 (he was killed on his birthday!), Jek Wen Shin, 7/11/76. Tremblingly my fingers opened the packets. Inside each was a strange-looking thing – a dead worm? a dried piece of intestine? each tied in the middle with a piece of lucky red string. I stared in puzzlement. What on earth was it? Then I knew. Umbilical cords. Or rather, the dried shrivelled remains of new-born babies' umbilical cords.

It was only later that I learnt from Boh Yuen the traditional Chinese practice of saving the cord of each new-born, usually a son. The mother, still in the throes of after-birth, treasuring the cord that had bound the child to her for nine months – I was moved by the symbolism.

Boh Yuen was rather vague when I asked him about the reason for the saving of this little bit of birth's detritus, and said it had something to do with parents' wish for success and prosperity for their sons in life.

I attended a simple temple ritual in which the three cords were burnt and thus ceremonially returned to the rightful owners. I could almost see the three spirits in joyful flight at last, winging home. So for months three little ghosts in my flat had been in torment to be reunited with their birth-cords. Did that mean they were going to be born again?

For their sakes, I hope so. I want to believe that wherever

they have gone, they will be free from those monstrous parents (especially the dastardly father) and they will have the good fortune to be born, in their second birth, to genuinely loving, caring parents. For I understand from Boh Yuen that in that other of the Chinese, the primary concerns of this world, such as eating, sleeping, living in comfortable houses, spending money, getting married, having children, etc. go on in much the same way.

Kamala says, pointing to the table with the two drawers, "Strange. How come we didn't see this when the men came to take away the furniture? Shall we get rid of it now?"

I say, "No, I'd like to keep it, if you don't mind."

Gentle into the Night

When old Madam Ong Sim Heok's favourite grandson, Benjy, was killed in a freak accident during a National Service training exercise, nobody dared to break the news to her. She was old and ill, and the shock of the news would surely kill her. The family hoped that she would go to a peaceful death unaware of the terrible tragedy.

So all the time that they were going through an unspeakable grief, they had to put on a brave face and attempt some jocularity in the face of the old lady's persistent questions. Why hadn't Benjy come to visit her for so long? Didn't he know she was ill? Was he too busy with friends and girlfriends to even drop in for a few minutes to see his old grandmother?

The family made all sorts of excuses on Benjy's behalf and told all kinds of lies, to pacify Madam Ong. They had to get together and work out a proper coordination of their lying, for the old lady, despite her years, was sharp and could detect inconsistencies straightaway. Once, she said to Benjy's mother, "How come you're telling me Benjy's in Taiwan for training when Lillian (Lillian was Benjy's sister) just said he's staying with 'Tiku' ('Tiku' was Benjy's best friend) preparing for some exams?" Then of course there had to be a quick scramble to undo the damage, offer fresh explanations, tell new lies to cover the old. Old Madam Ong frowned in vexed perplexity and suspicion. "I don't know what's going on," she said peevishly, "but you all had better stop making excuses for that young man and tell him to come and see his grandmother before she dies. Can't he even make a phone call?"

The story agreed on by the family was this: Benjy had been sent with some others to Taiwan for a special programme as part of the National Service training. It was a very stringent programme meant for only the best and most promising servicemen. They would not be allowed to contact their families, whether by writing or by phone. If they survived the training, they would be immediately promoted to very important positions. Benjy was enjoying the programme but missing everyone, especially Grandma. He had told a friend who had completed the programme and returned home to Singapore to send his love to Grandma and tell her that the first thing he would do back home would be to take her on the long-promised holiday to Canada.

The lie about Benjy's message through the friend was meant to comfort the old lady and bring a smile to her face. Doting on him, she liked to hear about his love for her. Before she went down with old age and illness, she regaled friends and relatives with an abundance of stories about her precious grandson, her fondness of him embellishing the stories extravagantly to his acute embarrassment. She liked in particular to tell about Benjy's promise to do this or that for his grandma. She had brought him up from infancy and the special bond between them was touching to see.

"What will you do when you grow up?" To the invariable adult question, the little boy's immediate reaction was to run and hug his grandmother and yell shrilly, "I'll build a big house for my Ma-Ma to stay in, and I'll be a policeman and shoot all those who steal Ma-Ma's handbag!" This was a reference to an incident when Madam Ong had her handbag snatched and suffered severe bruises grappling with the robber.

When Benjy was in secondary school, his grandmother one day told him about a friend of hers who had come back from a holiday in Canada, breathless with praise for the beautiful country. Immediately, the thirteen-year-old boy said solemnly, "As soon as I get a job after university, I'll start saving to take you for a holiday in Canada, Ma-Ma."

She wept when he left home to begin his National Service training, and worried endlessly about whether he would have enough to eat, suffer from poisonous insect bites in the jungle, suffer from the bullying of superiors, collapse in the hot sun, meet with an accident etc. Once she tried to sneak a packet of his favourite *nonya kueh* past the sentry, and was politely that no gifts of food were allowed.

On the day of Benjy's funeral, it was arranged that some relatives would stay with her and join in the family conspiracy of placating her with yet more elaborate lies.

Benjy's face had almost been blown off by a grenade in the freak accident. At the mortuary, his mother, looking upon the shattered face, had fainted. At the funeral, she fainted again and was held up by his father who looked ready to faint himself. His sister Lillian, aged fourteen, had suddenly become the strongest one in the family, running around doing the necessary things in a house of sudden mourning, making phone calls, answering calls, comforting her parents. As she prayed for the soul of her poor brother, she also prayed for their grandmother: "Please, God, don't let Ma-Ma know. Let her die peacefully."

But old Madam Ong Sim Heok refused to die without seeing her grandson. Her questions became more persistent and fretful. Then she became truly angry.

"I don't care what his National Service superiors say," she said, her face flushed with anger, as she lay on her deathbed, "but I want my grandson to come and see me right away. Don't they have any heart? An old lady is dying, and her beloved grandson can't get permission to come and see her! And don't you all have any guts, letting them get away with this?"

Madam Ong lay quietly for a while, plotting a strategy. "Lillian," she said, "I want you to do something at once. Write a letter on my behalf to the Prime Minister of Singapore. I want to go right to the top to complain! Maybe only then will those fools do something."

Lillian sat down and wrote the letter. Old Madam Ong signed it. She closed her eyes, heaved a deep sigh and murmured, "One shouldn't have to do these things on one's death-bed."

She was sinking rapidly. But the crying need to see her favourite grandson for the last time kept the remaining life flickering in her frail body, the continuing hope burning in her eyes.

A few days later, she appeared much calmer. Indeed the family noticed a peaceful, contented air about her.

"I knew it would work," she said. Her voice was growing weaker and Lillian, who happened to be the only one in the room then, had to bend down to put her ear close to the dying woman's mouth.

"Always go straight to the top with a complaint!" said the dying woman with spirit. She said that Benjy had grown much thinner and paler.

"When did you see him?" said Lillian. "When did he come?"

"Didn't you all know? Only this morning. He sat right here," she made a weak movement with her head to indicate a spot on the bed, beside her, "and he held my hand."

Old Madam Ong smiled contentedly. Then she suddenly opened her eyes and said with a worried look, "Lillian, he looked sad. He was covering part of his face with a piece of white cloth. I said, 'Benjy, why are you covering your face?' But he wouldn't remove the cloth. He wouldn't tell me anything. He just sat there, holding my hand and saying, 'Ma-Ma, I've come.'"

Lillian, unable to hold back her tears, continued listening with her ear almost pressed to her grandmother's mouth. She was already thinking, with an unbearable heaviness of heart, "I can't tell Mom this. It will break her heart." She would tell a lie if necessary. Lies to the dying about the dead. Lies to the living about the dying and the dead. They were part of the whole reality of coping. The dying needed to go gentle into the night.

Old Madam Ong, with a last flush on the rapidly failing flesh and a last gleam in the rapidly fading eyes, said, as happy memories rushed back and turned the last, almost inaudible whisper into a chuckle of joyous merriment, "He says he will be a policeman when he grows up to protect his grandmother from crooks! And he says he's saved enough money for our long journey together!"

The Ghost of Miss Daisy Ooi Mei Lang

Miss Daisy Ooi Mei Lang, the principal of Pin Yun Secondary School, was killed in a car accident at the junction of Dowling Road and Pek Moy road in 1987. She was excitedly testing her new Mazda when it began to rain heavily, and she drove straight into an oncoming truck, and was instantly killed.

For eight years, up till 1995, the ghost of Miss Ooi was seen in her school. The dead who are not aware that they have died are said to continue their habitual activities in familiar well-loved places on earth. Awareness, when it comes, is often extremely traumatic and is usually initiated by the living who then have the awesome responsibility of easing the confused ghost's entry into the other world.

Poor Miss Ooi was clearly not aware that she had died.

She had been in Pin Yun Secondary School as a student, a teacher and finally a principal, the principalship being the crowning achievement of a simple life of hard work and service to others. Miss Ooi never married, in order to be in a position to care for a household of old dependents, comprising her aged parents, aunt and godmother. Over the years they died, one by one, gradually freeing Miss Ooi to live her own life. But she remained single and channelled all her energies to the managing of her school, taking a personal pride in every aspect of its life, from the welfare of her staff and students, as well as that of the school clerks, cleaning woman, canteen operator, gardener and caretaker, to the cleanliness of the buildings and grounds. Miss Ooi would stay back till the evening, watching the students at their various extra-curricular activities of sports and games, and drive off home only after she had made sure everyone else has left. In her plain light-coloured blouse and dark-coloured skirt, sensible shoes, neat short hair and silver-rimmed glasses, she was a familiar figure in the school buildings and large sprawling compound, always doing her rounds of inspection with indefatigable energy. Her last act in the school, on a Saturday afternoon, was to alert the old gardener Vellu to the presence of a bee hive in one of the branches of a tree at the back of the school, and to make a note to remind herself to warn students at assembly on Monday morning.

On Sunday, she was killed in the accident.

On Monday, while her body was still lying in the coffin in the parlour of her home, attended by grieving relatives, friends and colleagues, her ghost was already seen in the school. It was the gardener Vellu who was the first to see her. Informed about her death only on Monday morning itself, after the school assembly when the vice-principal Mr Chionh had made the sad announcement to staff and students, Vellu looked puzzled and said, shaking his head, “No, no. I see Miss Ooi only just now. Miss Ooi walking there,” pointing to the spot near her office, “and she say ‘Good morning, Vellu.’” Pressed for further details, Vellu said she was in a white blouse and grey skirt and was carrying her usual flask of coffee and lunchbox of sandwiches.

Then it was the turn of the gardener, Mat. He said he had seen Miss Ooi standing near one of the flower-beds in the well-tended school garden, inspecting a row of cannas. He actually saw her bend down, and pinch off a dead leaf on a flower stalk. The cleaning woman Ah Moi was next. She ran to tell the vice-principal, her face ashen with shock, "She's in there, sitting at her desk," pointing to the principal's office.

By the time of her funeral, three days after the accident, the ghost of Miss Daisy Ooi Mei Lang had been seen by all th servants in the school. "Not surprising," said one of the teachers. "She was always going to the Ministry of Education or the Ministry of Labour to demand better wages or working conditions for them." The servants, though, were not exactly happy about the signal honour of being singled out by a ghost for first viewing. They looked nervous, whispering among themselves.

Then the teachers and students began to hear strange sounds. Walking along the corridors outside the classrooms, some of teachers would hear the familiar sound of Miss Ooi's footsteps, turn around sharply and see no one. Or the equally familiar sound of Miss Ooi blowing her nose into a handkerchief. She had sinus problems and always carried a neat white handkerchief in a skirt pocket. Sometimes they would smell her presence. Miss Ooi never used perfume in her life, but she often rubbed a certain very pungent-smelling embrocation oil on her elbows and knees, to relieve aches and pains. Once, during assembly, the distinctive smell of the oil filled the hall. For a few seconds, the staff and the students stood very still, not daring to move or say anything.

Only a handful of teachers, including the vice-principal Mr. Chionh, reported actually seeing Miss Ooi's ghost.

Mrs. Moreira, a science teacher, one morning saw Miss Ooi climbing up the stairs leading to the music room, easily recognising her by the blouse, skirt and hairstyle. The vice-principal said that one afternoon when he went into the principal's room (left vacant for months) to get something, he saw her standing by the window, looking out. A new student from a foreign country who came to the school nearly a year after Miss Ooi's death, reported seeing a lady who exactly matched her description, adjusting a chart hanging on the wall of her classroom.

Miss Ooi's ghost had so far been benign. But benign or not, a ghost's presence is seldom welcome. Two teachers had nervously asked for a transfer to another school; four parents had quietly removed their children. The new principal, a Mr. Seng Song Tee, decided, a month after his arrival, that the time had come to cleanse the school of the presence. The language used was gentle – "helping Miss Ooi's spirit find its way home." It was a decision at the purely private, unofficial level, since the Ministry of Education would not approve of anything that might be even remotely construed as a superstitious act, quite at odds with the secularism and rationalism of the society. Some trouble-maker might even write to the newspapers about it, and start a hullabaloo in the 'Forum' pages of the Straits Times, something that the Ministry would avoid at all cost. So Mr. Seng only privately informed a ministry official, in order, as he said, "to cover himself" should there be any inquiry later. He quietly informed only a few trusted members of the staff, the whole idea being to play down the event as much as possible, and speed up the resolution of an increasingly intolerable situation in his new school.

Miss Ooi had been a Taoist before she converted to the Catholic religion. So Mr. Seng, to play safe, arranged for two separate rituals, on two separate days, the first conducted by a priest from the Tau Sin Temple and the other by Father Rozario from the Church of St. Anne.

Mr. Seng had reason to regret his decision.

The ghost went berserk, clearly upset by what it must have regarded as an act of supreme effrontery – ousting a principal from her beloved school. Later one of the teachers recollected an incident, years back, when a junior official from the Ministry of Education had presumed to come to the school to criticise Miss Ooi about some aspect of the running of her school. Casting of her usual polite, genteel bearing, Miss Ooi turned a livid face upon the startled official and said, "You leave my school this instant." The rage was multiplied many times in her ghost; it went on a rampage of fury, so that for weeks, staff, students and servants heard loud angry noises, banging of doors, sudden crashing of pictures and maps to the floor, and on one occasion, a wild disarray of the furniture in the staff room. The caretaker reported seeing Miss Ooi, distressed, tearful, angry.

After the incident, nobody tried to get rid of Miss Ooi's ghost again. Mr. Seng hurriedly left the school. The new principal, a Mrs. Christina Liew, held a meeting specifically to tell her staff to be philosophical about it all, to accept the ghost in their midst, a ghost that after all harmed nobody and only wanted to be left alone to continue its habitual activities in beloved surroundings.

So the ghost of Miss Daisy Ooi Mei Lang was left alone in peace. She continued to be seen and heard, but never threw any tantrums again. Once somebody heard singing from the music room; nobody was found to be there, upon investigation. Miss Ooi, when happy, hummed a song or two.

In 1995, eight years after Miss Ooi's death, Pin Yun Secondary School was relocated to another district in Singapore, as part of a general upgrading programme by the Ministry of Education. The old school was razed to the ground; the new school, bearing the same name, was much bigger and smarter-looking, reflecting the sophistication of education in Singapore in the 90s, and boasting excellent, most up-to-date facilities such as a theatrette and a fully air-conditioned library.

The ghost of Miss Ooi remained in the old location, clearly unaware of the move. Somebody reported seeing a very confused ghost wandering around, looking lost and distressed. A principal suddenly bereft of her beloved school, the ghost almost went mad with the pain of the loss and bewilderment. But for the new Pin Yun, it was a relief. For the ghost did not find its way to the new school; it would have been intolerable for the new Pin Yun, gleaming in its newness, to be haunted by the ghost of a dead principal. Refusing to be exorcised, the ghost was forced, by the relocation, to stop its haunting.

The principal of the new Pin Yun was a Mrs. Bernadette Chan who instead of feeling relieved, felt very sorry. She had heard reports of the ghost trapped in its ignorance and confusion, wandering dazed among the razed remains of her beloved school. Somebody had seen her sitting on a pile of stones weeping inconsolably. Mrs. Bernadette Chan decided she had to do something.

She had never met Miss Ooi but understood the pain of deprivation and loss.

The decision to help relieve Miss Ooi's suffering and provide her a new home cost Mrs. Chan a cool ten thousand dollars which, with much effort, she managed to persuade the school's Board of Directors to approve as an item of necessary expenditure.

Today, a visitor shown round Pin Yun Secondary School may

be a little puzzled by a room that is always locked and that has, on its door, a plaque bearing the name of Miss Daisy Ooi Mei Lang in beautiful gold letters. Inside it seems, the room is tastefully furnished, with the desk that Miss Ooi used to sit at when she was principal. Nearby is a cupboard of various trophies won by the school during the years of her principalship, including the first prize for a national oratorical contest for which Miss Ooi had personally coached the school representatives. On the wall are familiar, loved pictures, including one, framed in silver, of a staff picture taken in 1985, which was supposedly Miss Ooi's favourite.

Her ghost, wandering in misery and confusion on the old site of Pin Yun Secondary School, had been gently led in a ceremony conducted by a Catholic priest (Mrs. Chan figured that the Taoism, renounced for the new religion, probably no longer counted) to the new site, and formally invited to occupy her new home. Miss Ooi's ghost resides in the room and is apparently very contented there. Very occasionally the sound of her footsteps moving about is heard, and the sniffling into a handkerchief, but mostly it is happy humming.

Mrs. Bernadette Chan is reluctant to talk about this room specially set up in her school for the ghost of Miss Daisy Ooi Mei Lang. All she will say, with a smile, is: "That was the least I could do."

The Seventh Day

Both my son, who graduated from Harvard with a degree in Physics, and my daughter, who is a physiotherapist, are amused when I tell them the story of my Uncle Botak who died years before they were born.

"Surely you're not serious, Dad," says Brandon.

"Everything's ultimately explainable in terms of the human mind," says Desiree. "Anyone can see that it was a case of pure auto-suggestion, Dad. You wanted something to happen; your mind caused it to happen."

The young are certainly entitled to their scepticism. In my youth, I had, my share of it, keeping it hidden from my aunt, who was the greatest devotee of temple deities and who regularly made me drink blessed temple water and wear all kinds of amulets on red strings round my neck or wrist to ward off evil spirits. I submitted to all her ministrations because I knew they were driven by loving concern.

No aunt ever loved an orphaned nephew more. Indeed, my status as the fatherless and motherless waif drew a special tenderness of pity from my kind-hearted aunt who made it a practice, during meal-times, to pick out the best parts of the meat and vegetables with her chopsticks and transfer them onto my plate, much to the resentment of my cousin Ah Siong.

I loved Aunt dearly, but my special affection was reserved for my Uncle Botak. His nickname had less to do with a deficiency of hair than his preferred style of a close crew-cut throughout his life. Uncle Botak was a large, hearty, amiable, fun-loving man who ran a small dry goods shop in our *kampung*. In his free time, he liked to wander about the *kampung*, talking to fellow villagers, exchanging news, taking part in any activity that promised excitement and fun, such as helping to capture and kill a huge python that had been eating the villagers' chickens and even piglets, and helping to nab an intruder from a nearby town, who had been peeping at the *kampung* women bathing at the well.

Uncle Botak took me along on these excursions, which I enjoyed thoroughly. Once, I played truant, sneaking out of the school to join him in a fishing expedition in a jungle river. When Aunt found out, she scolded us severely, and tweaked my ear until I howled. "You will study hard and get a good education and earn a good living," she said sternly. "Why can't you be like Ah Siong?" My cousin never gave Aunt any trouble; he always scored good grades in school.

After the scolding, Aunt made Uncle and me drink some brew made from the holy temple water and joss-stick ashes, that were supposed to negate the harmful effects of our expedition, for Aunt believed that the jungle teemed with malignant spirits ready to punish those who dared to disturb their abodes in rivers, ponds, swamps, trees or bushes. As Uncle Botak and I meekly drank the holy brew, he turned round and gave me a wink. Sometimes he made fun of Aunt's superstitiousness but never in her presence.

Tall, burly, with a booming voice, he was the gentlest person

I knew. He was in constant dread of displeasing his strong-willed wife, yet loved her dearly. In a *kampung* full of women who complained about their husband's brutality, infidelity or idleness, Uncle Botak was the ideal husband. He would comply with Aunt's every wish and endure any amount of inconvenience on her account, once scouring several marketplaces to find a special pristine kind of young fowl that Aunt needed for her offering to a revered temple deity who would accept nothing less than virginal pullet, steamed in its own pure juices and offered with joss-sticks and flowers.

When it was time for me to go to secondary school, Uncle Botak bought me a bicycle, as the nearest school was miles away from the *kampung*. Then when I finished my secondary education, Uncle and Aunt scraped together whatever savings they had to send me to university. They could even afford to let me board in one of the university's hostels for students. My cousin Siong had fortunately won a government scholarship, which meant that the spare money could go to me. I would work at part-time jobs during the vacations to earn some money to enable me to buy gifts for Uncle and Aunt.

When the *kampung* was cleared by the government for industrial development, Uncle grew very depressed. He did not like living in the small, crammed flat on the twelfth storey of a block of the government-built flats that he had been given as part of the resettlement programme. He missed the *kampung* and its wide open spaces terribly. Only six months after moving into the new home, Uncle suffered a stroke, which over the months, reduced him to half his size. But he tried to be cheerful whenever I came to visit. We would talk about our happy carefree *kampung* days.

In my third year at university, Uncle Botak died. Cousin

Siong, who had gone abroad on a post-graduate scholarship, flew back in time for the funeral. Aunt was distraught, although she had been expecting his death in the last few months when he had hardly moved from his bed.

Something kept up Aunt's spirits during the bereavement. It was the prospect of welcoming back Uncle's ghost seven days after his death. All her energies were channelled into the preparation for this special homecoming. Like her ancestors, she faithfully observed the custom of meticulous, loving preparation, sweeping and cleaning his bedroom, putting clean sheets on the bed, clean pillow and bolster cases, clean towels. She set up a table with a mug of his favourite tea, a pot of boiled rice, and a bowl and a pair of chopsticks beside it. Her ancestors in China had been even more painstaking in their preparations, spreading a thin layer of ash on the floor, so as to allow the returning ghost to leave its footprints, the surest proof of its return.

Aunt was in a fever of activity and expectation. It was hr way of coping with the pain of her bereavement. Indeed, she was brimming with so much confidence that expectation became certainty. "Prawn noodles," she said reflectively. "It was his favourite, you know. Maybe I should get ready a plate of prawn noodles too."

There was one moment when the confidence faltered and she turned to me to say, a little anxiously, "Do you think he'll come?" I put a reassuring arm on her shoulder. Cousin Siong had left two days after the funeral and would therefore not be around for his father's return. I wished I were in his position, if only to be spared the disappointment on Aunt's face on the morning after the seventh day. She would see the room exactly as she had laid it out, and would have to pretend, for her own consolation, that the ghost had returned. I remember that as a boy I once heard her talk about a relative's joy in seeing all the evidence of her dead husband's return – the crumpled bedsheet, the hollow in the pillow where the ghost had laid his head, the footprints on the floor where he had walked, even without the aid of strewn ash. Uncle Botak and I had listened politely; then he turned around and gave me one of his merry winks.

Sitting alone in my room, thinking sadly of Uncle lying cold and still in his grave, I suddenly had an idea. It was an idea born of a decision to do everything in my power to ensure that Aunt would get her dearest wish. Uncle had never disappointed her in life; now I would make sure that through me, he would not disappoint her in death either. It was as if the spirit of Uncle Botak, as kind and thoughtful as ever, had suggested the idea to me.

On the evening of the seventh day, when everybody was asleep, I stole into the room prepared for Uncle's return. Lying down on the bed to crease and crumple the sheets, leaving a conspicuous hollow in the pillow, shifting the pillow bolster to a new position on the bed, drinking some of the tea in the mug, picking up the chopsticks to stir the smooth surface of the boiled rice in the pot and perhaps leave a few grains in the bowl – all these would take just a few minutes.

I stole out of my room and entered Uncle's dark, silent room. I was immediately seized by a strange sensation that I was not alone. It came suddenly, real, palpable. I stood very still in the darkness, not daring to breathe. A cold, numbing chill began spreading through my body. There should have been no fear: alive, Uncle Botak had been the friendliest, most reassuring presence; dead, he should be no different. My heart was pounding wildly.

I heard sounds. They were the sounds of someone walking in the room with bare feet. It was a hurried, restless kind of movement, conveying agitation. There came more sounds in the dense darkness, a cough, a rough clearing of phlegm in the throat, a grunt, the tiny thud of a small object dropped on the floor. I stood still in a paralysis of terror.

Then it all happened – so fast that I seemed no longer in control but was being borne along by someone else's will. I felt strong hands grasping my shoulders, propelling me to the bed and forcing me to lie down. As I lay trembling, I felt the same pair of strong hands moving my head and legs this way and that, adjusting them to the contours of the pillow and bolster. Lying very still, I continued to hear the scuffling, breathing, coughing sounds, now amplified by closeness. At one point, the sounds were so close that they became a roaring tumult in my brain. Then I felt an enormous weight on my chest, as if somebody were sitting on it. Next I felt the pair of hands again, pushing me up and towards the table where Aunt had put the pot of rice and the mug of tea. I do not remember what happened next, except that I felt something like a wet pad hit my face. I stumbled, hit the table and heard chopsticks rolling off and falling to the floor. I got up and ran gasping out of the room.

I stayed awake all night wondering about what had happened. Sufficiently calm, I began to think of possible explanations. A dream? A hallucination? People under tremendous stress have been known to have the strangest experiences. After all, I had been under considerable strain not only of mourning Uncle's death but worrying about Aunt's pain.

The far from benign presence was puzzling. The air had practically crackled with the hostility. This could not have been my friendly, warm, kind Uncle Botak. Death is said to have a softening influence even on the hardest, most unfeeling people, transforming them into gentle, well-disposed spirits. Had it had the opposite effect in Uncle's case? Or was Uncle still his same benign self but deliberately putting on a show of great displeasure at my presumptuousness in doubting Aunt's faith in him, and determined to teach me a lesson?

Or was that presence in the room someone else, someone who died at the same time but had been denied the seventh day welcome home, so that he had come back as an interloper, appropriating another's welcome?

My head reeled with all the surmising and began to throb painfully. I was certain of one thing. The experience had been real and not imaginary. I could still hear the sounds of the footsteps and the coughing in my ears, still feel the pressure of the hands on my shoulders. I did something for proof. I removed my shirt and examined my shoulders in the mirror.

There were distinct marks on them.

Throughout the night, I heard, coming from the distance, the mourning howling of dogs, long, melancholy, drawn-out wails that added to my terror which shaped into a great sadness so that I found myself sobbing uncontrollably.

Aunt said the next morning, after the inspection of the room, "He's come back. I knew he would." Bright tears glistened in her eyes. In those days, she wept easily, whether from pain or joy. Like Uncle, she missed the *kampung* and hated the small, crammed flat but would live in it for another twenty years.

My son Brandon says, "Strange, Dad, but I still think it was an entirely *subjective* experience."

My daughter Desiree says, "Don't you see, dad, you were scared to do it, but wanted to do it so badly, so subconsciously you shifted the responsibility to a ghost. Ghosts are convenient means for lots of people to resolve their inner conflicts, fears, needs, longings."

As I say the young are entitled to their scepticism.

Elemental

I am a collector of what must be the most bizarre collectibles in the world – newspaper reports of lovers who dies together in a suicide pact. I show the fine care and systematic meticulousness of the serious collector, arranging my material into suitable categories, labelling and showcasing these, meeting with fellow collectors to talk, discuss, exchange thoughts about what must be the most drastic of human decisions. Unfortunately – very fortunately, considering the highly questionable nature of this past-time – there are not many collectibles or collectors around. I have only a thin, five-page file of the reports and I know of only one person, a fellow journalist for The Courier, who shares the same morbid interest, but says he will certainly not raise it to the unhealthy level of an obsession.

My 'collection' started more than thirty years ago. In 1965, when I was a teenager in school, I read about a suicide pact between two young lovers, which gripped my imagination so much that it became the subject of an intense poem I wrote for my school magazine. The boy, aged nineteen, and the girl, aged seventeen, one night drove off in a rented car, parked it along a lonely lane far from their homes, locked themselves in, poured kerosene over their bodies and set themselves ablaze. I remember vividly the picture in the newspaper of the charred car, all twisted and blackened metal, and the remains of the couple that had been brought out, aid on the ground and hurriedly covered with a piece of tarpaulin.

The report mentioned the parental opposition, from both sides, to the young couple's relationship, which must have been the direct cause of their despair and suicide. I suppose it was the Romeo and Juliet element of tragic, star-crossed young love that had made the story of Ricky Ong Phui Nam and Molly Tay Min Hwee so unforgettable for me.

In 1972, when I was an undergraduate in the university, I read about another suicide pact, this time of a couple, both aged twenty, who went up to the thirteenth floor of a high-rise block of apartments, some distance from where they lived, tied their wrists together with a silk scarf, and plunged together to their deaths. The smashed bodies of Sanjay Das and Neo Swee Ping lying on the ground could not have been less horrifying than the pile of blackened cinders that had been poor Ricky and Molly. They had left a joint suicide note to their respective parents; again it appeared to be a case of young love blighted by parental opposition.

In 1986, the Chinese language newspapers carried a report (somehow the event was ignored by the English language newspapers) of a couple – the man was a businessman, aged thirty-five and married, and the girl, a factory worker, aged twenty-two, unmarried, living with her widowed mother – who had one night waded into the sea together and drowned.

Mr. Tan Kim Seng and Miss Wong Gek Boey too, had had their wrists tied together with a red handkerchief. (I had wondered about the romantic symbolism of this last act of physical togetherness. Or perhaps it was just a simple means of ensuring there would be no changing of mind at the last moment by either party, no breaking free of a sacred last vow.) No bleak picture accompanied the report, but a cheerful one of the couple, in some happier time, clad in warm clothes atop a snowy hill, on an illicit holiday together in a far-off country.

Fire, earth, water – I was suddenly struck by the elemental aura surrounding the lovers' deaths, investing them with a certain terrible dignity and power. I saw the different suicides, happening years apart from each other, suddenly come together in an awesome display of the human connectedness with the elements from which we arose from primeval chaos.

Only one element was missing – air. And I felt a strange *frisson* of terror in 1989 when I read about another suicide pact that completed the terrifying picture of love's despair acted out in the vast churning background of elemental chaos. A pilot and his mistress committed suicide together when the plane he was flying deliberately changed course, crashed into a mountain side and exploded, hurtling one hundred other souls into the pitiless void of air and down into the equally pitiless denseness of jungle and mangrove swamp.

It was only at a later stage of the official inquiry into the crash that the truth emerged. The pilot, Captain Lam Yew Boon, had apparently incurred immense debts through gambling; his wife, who had discovered the affair, had started divorce proceedings; both his teenage children had openly repudiated him; his mistress, Miss Maggie Oon Han Mee who was herself in debt, was passionately in love with him and had insisted on marriage, which he did not want. In the end, the beleaguered couple planned a suicide. The plan would never have been known if the mistress had not left a hurried note to her sister, which was brought up in the official inquiry. There was such an outpouring of rage from the grief-stricken families of the hundred innocent victims that, for a while, the pilot's family, even though they were totally blameless, had to go into hiding. The wife became a special target of opprobrium when it was thought that she had benefited from the tragedy by a huge sum of insurance money. In the end, very quietly, she and her children left to settle in Australia. Miss Ong's sister too, disappeared from public view.

For weeks after the results of the inquiry were made public, the bereaved ones asked again and again, in outraged anguish, "If they wanted to die, why couldn't they have just died on their own? Why did they have to kill one hundred others?"

Today, ten years later, the ghosts of Captain Lam and his mistress Maggie Oon are said to be roaming around the earth still, in punishment for their unspeakably evil deed. Villagers living near the site of the crash, report seeing, on certain nights, the distraught figures of a man and a woman, fitting the description of the pilot and his mistress (he was tall with strong features, she was slim and slight, with long, straight hair). They were always reported as looking lost and confused, wandering aimlessly about under trees or struggling in the swamps. One villager reportedly actually coming face to face with them; he said they looked pale and frightened, opening and closing their mouths in a wordless appeal for help. He fled screaming.

Another villager, with some friends on a night hunting expedition, saw the couple under a tree weeping together. Their wails were taken up by a sudden rush of cold wind and carried over a great distance, reverberating in the night air and heard by people for miles around. Over the years, the villagers have come to live with these strange occurrences and not be bothered by them. They say the time will come when the ghosts have fully paid for their crime and will be allowed to rest in peace at last.

The full payment of the crime will take another ten years at least. This is the confident assessment of Madam Low Ngin Hoong whose son, daughter-in-law and four-year-old grandson had perished in the crash. She says that the fortune-teller whom she had consulted shortly after the tragedy told her that the combined strength of the curses hurled at the wicked pair by the grieving relatives of the victims, was a truly powerful elemental force capable of breaking through the barrier separating the worlds of the living and the dead, and of dragging out the ghosts of the guilty dead for punishment. The powerful force continues to operate on the ghosts of the pilot and his mistress, condemning them to a hell on the face of the earth itself, where they will wander helplessly about in the site of their heinous deed, for years and years, long after the soul of their victims have gone on to a peaceful rest, long after the souls of their fellow suicides in fire, water and earth, have paid for their self-inflicted deaths and gone, too, to their rest.

Madam Low Ngin Hoong says, with still a tinge of bitterness, "I know I should forgive the dead, but forgiveness does not come easy to a heart that continues to bleed, even after so many years." One day, she says, she will go to the site of the tragic deaths of her family, to bury the bitterness. But not before the elemental power of combined sorrow and anger of those sad days has worked itself out at last and permitted the release, from their torment, of the ghosts of Captain Lam Yew Boon and Miss Maggie Oon Han Mee.

The Child

"My daughter, are you well?"

"My mother, I am well."

"My daughter, do you have enough to eat?"

"Yes, Mother. I am eating well."

"My daughter, take good care of yourself."

"I will, Mother."

For years, Ah Cheng Soh had been going to the Hai Thong Temple to speak to her dead daughter, Ah Lian, through one of the temple mediums. Ah Lian had died in infancy, during the Japanese Occupation, when desperate mothers, too poor to buy milk for their babies, fed them sugar water. Ah Cheng Soh's husband and brother had been killed by Japanese soldiers. A few months later, the poor young widow saw her sickly, undernourished baby die in her arms, thus losing three loved ones in the terrible war. Continuing to make rice dumplings to sell in the market, after the war was over, Ah Cheng Soh eked out a modest livelihood, living by herself in a tiny, one-room flat in an old block of flats (one of the first to be built in Singapore, and since then torn down to make way for taller, more modern-looking blocks with better facilities).

While her dead husband and brother had long been

consigned to oblivion, being remembered only once a year when the Feast of the Hungry Ghosts came around, her little infant daughter remained dear and close through regular contact via the temple medium. Ah Cheng Soh kept watch, like any loving mother, on the child's progress in the other world she had gone to, for there too, babies become children and children grow into adults. When little Ah Lian was four years old, Ah Cheng Soh bought a paper doll and other paper toys from a shop selling gifts for the dead, and burnt these in a temple for proper delivery to the deceased daughter. Two years later, Ah Cheng Soh, with the same motherly indulgence, sent up a gift of a tricycle, beautifully done in multi-coloured paper, complete with a delightful tricycle bell in the front. When Ah Lian was twelve years old, her mother brought her a pair of ear-rings, exquisitely made with fine gold paper. Ah Cheng Soh thought, with a sad heart, that if her daughter had lived, that would be the age of the piercing of her ear-lobes and the wearing, for the first time, of gold jewellery to mark the imminence of womanhood.

"My daughter, are you well? Are you taking good care of yourself?"

This was Ah Lian's fourteenth year, and surely she would have had her first menses. Ah Cheng Soh worried about the difficulties the girl might be experiencing in her initiation into adulthood.

Her worst anxieties were confirmed. Ah Lian seemed confused and unhappy. The temple medium through whom she spoke to her mother, did not seem at all at ease, once or twice even heaving the immense sighs of an overcharged heart. When Ah Lian turned sixteen, her unhappiness was so great, it overflowed in tears. Ah Cheng Soh watched in alarm as big drops of tears oozed out of the medium's tightly closed eyes and splattered her cheeks.

"Oh, I can't bear it, I can't bear it," cried poor Ah Cheng Soh, weeping herself.

"My daughter, tell me what you want."

"My mother, find me a husband."

So the cause of the poor girl's distress, which she had been so reluctant to reveal, was loneliness. Alone in the vast drear world of the dead, the girl yearned for a male companion. Ah Cheng Soh immediately set about the task of finding her a spouse. She remembered that some years ago, a woman in the neighbourhood had gone on a similar search for her dead son who had also died in infancy and appeared in a dream, nineteen years later, to make his urgent request. The woman had managed to locate a couple whose little daughter, having died fifteen years ago, would now be about the right age for the young man. A marriage was subsequently arranged and solemnised in a temple that had conducted many such ghost marriages, where the bridal couple was usually represented by paper effigies, the wedding guests ate and drank as at any normal wedding party, and gifts of clothes, furniture, household utensils, jewellery, cash, etc. in ghost paper, were presented, being burnt to ashes and thus delivered to the couple.

Ah Cheng Soh began asking around for a suitable husband for her daughter. There had not been many deceased male infants who would have reached adulthood at this time but Ah Cheng Soh persisted, determined to make her daughter happy. At last, on the recommendation of someone, she took a bus long ride to another part of the city, and managed to find an old, blind woman living in an old folks' home, whose grandson had died in infancy and would now be about twenty years old.

The old woman gave her consent readily. The young man was consulted through the temple medium. He expressed his joy in the prospect of being united in marriage to Ah Lian.

Relieved and excited, Ah Cheng Soh began to prepare for the marriage of her daughter. It was a very simple ceremony as she could not afford anything beyond the gift of an *ang pow* each to the temple medium who had conveyed both the crucial request from her daughter and the eager assent of the young man, and the temple priest who conducted the ceremony, chanting prayers and burning joss-sticks. Two long strips of yellow prayer paper bearing the names and ages represented the couple; a modest offering of steamed chicken, noodles, oranges and sweetmeats, represented the wedding feast. But Ah Cheng Soh made sure there was cash in abundance for the couple to spend, burning a huge pile of ghost money.

Ah Cheng Soh's neighbours who knew about the marriage, congratulated her and offered good wishes, expressing warm thanks for her friendly sharing of the wedding food which she had brought back from the temple.

"My daughter, are you happy?"

"My mother, I am very happy. I thank you for your love and kindness, my mother."

One morning, at six, as Ah Cheng Soh opened the door of her little flat to take her rice dumplings to sell in the market, as had been practice these many years, she saw a bundle of something at her doorstep, saw it move and heard small sounds from it. She bent down to look. It was a new-born baby, wrapped in a white towel. Uttering little cries of astonishment, Ah Cheng Soh picked up the baby and carried it in her arms, gently rocking it. It was a baby girl, and it could not be more than a few days old. Ah Cheng Soh's first thought was to get some milk and warm clothes for the baby, her second thought was to go to the police and make a report. Hurrying back into her flat to get the baby out of the cold morning air, Ah Cheng Soh froze in the shock of a sudden realisation: *it was exactly nine months after the marriage of her daughter.* She stared at the tiny infant in her arms: This was her grand-daughter. A ghost child, but her grand-child nevertheless. Weakened by her shock, Ah cheng Soh sat down heavily on a chair, still carrying the baby wrapped in the towel.

The events in the days that followed were too much for poor Ah Cheng Soh to assimilate into her simple, even existence, and she went in a dazed state from one event to the next, gasping, hardly coherent, certain of only one thing so that even in her confusion she asserted the truth confidently, even aggressively, to the police and her neighbours, "I tell you this is my grand-child." The police had insisted on taking the child away to a hospital and making a search for the mother, necessary and correct procedures in a case like this. They were convinced that the mother was an earthly one, probably one of those factory girls foolish enough to get pregnant and desperate enough to leave their babies at other people's doorsteps or even throw them down garbage chutes or into rubbish bins.

"No, no," said Ah Cheng Soh, "I tell you it's my grandchild. Nine months. Nine months exactly. How can you explain that?"

She went to the temple medium for confirmation.

"My daughter, is it my grand-daughter?"

"My mother, it is."

To her great joy, the police search was unsuccessful and she was allowed to adopt the baby. By the time all the necessary formalities had been gone through with the police and the hospital authorities, the baby girl was already six months old. Ah

Cheng Soh was thrilled to bring her home. She paid somebody to sell her dumplings for her at the market, so that she could stay home and look after the baby.

"My daughter, what name would you and her father like to give her?"

"It is your wish, my mother."

Ah Cheng Soh named the baby "Poh Kim", meaning "Precious Gold", for no child brought greater joy to a lonely woman than this grand-child born of a daughter thought to have been lost forever nearly twenty years ago. The trouble came from the neighbours. They looked uneasy at the 'ghost baby' and would not let their children go near her. They whispered among themselves, sharing their strange observations about the strange baby who cried differently from other babies, who sprouted teeth well before the normal time, who, even at that very young age, looked at people with a strange look that made them turn away, their arms suddenly covered with goosebumps. Ah Cheng Soh's assistant at her dumplings stall in the market confided in frightened whispers, that she once held the baby and found herself bearing immense weight that got heavier and heavier until her arms almost gave way, and she had to quickly return the baby to its cradle.

When the child started to walk, one neighbour claimed that one day, as she looked at the child's feet, she noticed that they were not touching the ground, the surest proof of ghosthood. Another neighbour who lived next door said that every time the child cried in the night, a response came through the dark silence, in the form of a mournful wail of a dog, a melancholy hoot of an owl, a sighing of the wind or, on one occasion, a distinct cry from another ghost child.

As the whispered rumours spread, nobody ventured near

Ah Cheng Soh's flat. Walking along the common corridor, the neighbours quickened their steps as they passed her door and heaved a big sigh of relief when they did not have to look upon the ghost child who seemed to like sitting on the doorstep, playing with her toys or simply watching people pass by. She was a very quiet child, with large, gentle eyes that could fix themselves for a long time on others, much to their alarm. Unlike other children, she made hardly any noise, sitting by herself on the doorstep, watching everybody and everything with her large, intense, wistful eyes.

"If you look close enough," shuddered a neighbour, "you'll notice that the eyes are different. There's something very strange about them."

Ah Cheng Soh said to her grand-daughter, "My little Poh Kim, don't worry about what people say. You are my precious grand-daughter, a gift from my daughter." Ah Cheng Soh claimed that since the arrival of the child, all the aches and pains in her body had disappeared. Moreover, her dumplings business had improved vastly.

The neighbours were less happy. When the next door woman's son fell ill, the blame was immediately laid on the ghost child. "My Bah-Bah broke away from me and ran to her. I pulled him back immediately. But it was too late. He fell ill that very night."

In spite of their hostility, the neighbours did not dare scold or harm the ghost-child, fearing powerful recrimination. A man was said to have gone raving mad and died a horrible death for just uttering some insulting words to a ghost.

"My daughter, people are saying bad things about Poh Kim."

"My mother, do not worry. Her father and I watch over her and protect her."

One day, while the little girl, now aged three, was sitting on the doorstep, playing with a plastic cup and spoon, a man who lived in the neighbouring estate and who had heard of the ghost child, walked slowly up to her. He approached with much cautious and gentle deference. He squatted down in front of her and held out a handful of brightly coloured sweets. Poh Kim stared at them, then at him, fixing her large eyes on his face.

"Here, take them," coaxed the man, smiling. He pulled out of his pocket a doll with yellow hair, a red dress and bright pink shoes, and held it out to Poh Kim. She did not move but continued staring at him, then the doll. He patiently waited for her obvious interest in the gift to overcome her shyness. It finally did. She stirred slightly, then stretched out her hand for the doll.

"Good girl," said the man. Then he brought out of a paper bag a little ceramic jar filled with wooden sticks with numbers carved on them.

"Do this," said the man, and he demonstrated the requested action by giving the jar a few vigorous shakes. He handed the jar to the child. As if aware of the obligation to return a favour, she took the jar and shook it as required. Some of the sticks fell out. The man scooped them up eagerly, noting the numbers on them, then he went away.

Soon a rumour spread through the neighbourhood, provoking so much interest that is spread through other neighbourhoods as well, accruing so much power that it brought people flocking to its source. For the man who had gone to the ghost-child to get a winning number in the four-digits lottery, had won first prize with the number and become immensely rich overnight. Neighbours gaped at his new clothes, new gold watch, new house, new mistress, half his age. At a dinner party which he gave in the town's best restaurant to celebrate his fortune, he had revealed its source.

Ah Cheng Soh shooed away the neighbours who came flocking to her door, clutching jars, canisters, boxes, containing numbered sticks, begging to see her grand-child, trying to entice the child with gifts of toys and sweets, and the grandmother with promises of a sharing of certain wealth.

"A lucky child," they whispered among themselves. "The ghost-child is a lucky child."

About the Author

Catherine Lim is internationally recognised as one of the leading figures in the world of Asia fiction. The prolific writer and commentator has penned more than 20 books across various genres—short stories, novels, reflective prose, poems and satirical pieces. Many of her works are studied in local and foreign schools and universities, and have been published in various languages in several countries.

Also by Catherine Lim

Fiction

Deadline for Love

A Leap of Love

A Shadow of a Shadow of a Dream

The Catherine Lim Collection

The Bondmaid

The Teardrop Story Woman

Following the Wrong God Home

The Song of Silver Frond

Miss Seetoh in the World

Non-Fiction

Roll Out the Champagne, Singapore!

A Watershed Election: Singapore's GE 2011

An Equal Joy